THE KID WHO BEAT WALL STREET

and Saved Africa

COMPLETE EDITION

by Ginger Heller

Contact: Ginger Heller, consultant
P.O. Box 5015
Greenwich, Connecticut 06831

www.gingerheller.com

This book is a work of fiction. All characters, names, events and most places have been
created in the mind of the author. Any references to real locales are used fictitiously.

ISBN 13: 9781505570977
ISBN 10: 1505570972

For Donald, My Husband

My biggest supporter from the first day forward; he has helped me beyond all measure. Donald, by nature is a person of vision; wise, yet daring. He is a deep thinker with the ability to see the trees as well as the forest. He considers himself lucky, yet it is I who is lucky, for he is my love, and my own North Star.

THE KID
WHO BEAT
WALL STREET
and Saved Africa

COMPLETE EDITION

TABLE OF CONTENTS

PART II

PART III

� ✧ ✧

ACKNOWLEDGEMENTS

APPENDICES

THE KID WHO BEAT WALL STREET

and Saved Africa

COMPLETE EDITION

Prologue

Africa

Immediately Hakim knew. The men were kidnappers. He had heard about these bands of thugs who were snatching young boys and forcing them to become part of the militia, to become one of the vicious child soldiers of the region.

He had been searching for healing herbs in the nearby undergrowth when he saw them. Two were carrying rifles and the third, a tall man, had a machete tucked into his belt and a green bandana around his forehead. They all wore camouflage patterned military fatigues. The tall one was standing while talking to the others and swinging a burlap sack in a big circle around his head. The sack wasn't really that big; just big enough.

Instinctively, Hakim, a lanky fourteen-year-old boy, crouched down low and hid himself in the tall grass. He looked out over the plains below and studied the scene cautiously. There was a khaki jeep nearby. He moved into a position where he was in line with the jeep and hidden from the men.

"Ah," he gasped.

A boy was tied behind the jeep, tied and bound with a thick rope to the fender of the vehicle. The boy couldn't be more than ten or eleven years old, and he looked to be asleep.

Hakim lay down and flattened his body against the earth. Then he started to crawl towards the jeep, a hundred yards away. Two birds darted out from under the brush. He froze for a moment, then continued. The tall grasses created a perfect cover for a while, but after that he had to crawl out onto the open savanna. He was careful to keep the jeep between the men and himself so that he would not be in their line of vision. Slowly, ever so slowly, he crept. When he reached the vehicle, the boy was still asleep.

Hakim moved close to him, and then with a sudden thrust, he clamped his hand over the boy's mouth. The boy instantly awoke. Hakim, keeping his hand firmly pressed, looked into the lad's eyes. The fear was palpable.

"Shh," said Hakim. "Don't say a word. All right?" The boy nodded. Hakim untied him and told him to crawl back to the tall grasses and the wooded area, pointing in the direction from which he had come.

"And then run; run as fast as you can," he whispered. The boy nodded and was quickly gone.

Hakim watched him creep the hundred yards towards the tall grass. As the boy neared the edge of the woods, he stood up and then started to run. Immediately Hakim strode out from behind the truck and walked rapidly in the opposite direction.

"Hey, look at that kid," said one of the men. "Let's get him!" The three men took off running.

Though he was barefoot, Hakim started to run. He ran fast. He flew across the savanna. He ran like the wind.

Two of the men were not very fast, but the third one, the thin athletic man with the green bandana, was gaining. He was taller than Hakim, his legs were longer, his stride was wider.

Hakim could hear the man's strained breath behind him as he dashed towards the path that curved up a slight hill. When he reached the top of the ridge, he looked down. With only a moment's hesitation, he dove off the cliff like an eagle in flight. The river was clear and it was cold. He swam without stopping for a full ten minutes.

The thin man stood atop of the precipice and looked down. When the others reached him, they looked puzzled.

"Why'd you let him go?" one asked.

The thin man shrugged. "Can't swim."

PART I

1

"Awesome! Just awesome!"

Ten Thousand Dollars

Illinois, USA

IT COULDN'T BE A LIE BECAUSE IT SAID IT RIGHT THERE ON the computer screen. *$10,000.*

The numbers seemed to dance, even glow, as twelve year old Marco Polo Blackberry stared at them. His eyes grew wide when he finally realized what those five digits actually meant. He had just made a fortune. He was *rich*. And he had done it all in only one week.

He sat back in his chair, ran his fingers through his hair, and let out a long breath. Downstairs, he could hear the high-pitched voices of whatever cartoon his little sister was watching; but other than that, everything was silent.

He had been very careful to type the address he wanted, having long since learned that websites weren't of much use if you didn't put the address in accurately. He had even reminded himself to spell *Garrett* with two r's and two t's. Now he studied the computer screen closely. Yes, he had typed everything correctly; in the top, left-hand corner were the words: *White and Garrett Brokerage Firm.*

His heart started to pound. He wanted to open his bedroom window and shout at the top of his lungs. He wanted to jump around his room and punch the air with his fists, even run around the neighborhood and tell anyone who would listen. In fact he wanted the entire school, the whole world, to know what had just happened.

But Marco didn't do any of those things. Instead, he sat there quietly, listening to the cartoon playing in the family room. He was thinking deeply. Then a smile crept slowly across his face.

He had just made $10,000 on the Internet!

He crossed his legs and clasped his hands behind his neck. Then he leaned back in the chair. Visions floated in front of his eyes, visions of the largest flat screen panel TV, one that would take up an entire wall of his room; visions of that Jet Star ski board and, maybe a nice trip to the Colorado Mountains— just to try it out. Right now he was deeply immersed in these very pleasant thoughts.

Marco was, in fact, a deep thinker, though he would never classify himself as that. His height and weight were average, and he had mousey brown hair of the most ordinary kind with, the exception of a difficult cowlick that would sometimes rise up as if it had a will of its own. Yes, one might say, "ordinary," yet there was nothing ordinary about Marco.

At this moment though, he was incredibly happy… but something was gnawing at him. He didn't know what it was. A strange feeling blossomed in the pit of his stomach as thoughts raced through his brain. How could anything possibly be wrong?

Then it occurred to him, and he sighed. He was facing a very big problem.

✯ ✯ ✯

At school the next day, Marco pushed himself forward in his chair, then back, then forward, and then back again. Every few minutes, he turned and glanced at the large clock in the rear of the classroom, hearing very little of the wisdom his teacher was trying to impart.

When the lunch bell finally rang, he bounded into the hall, the smile on his face growing larger as he saw his friend, Joey, approaching. Joey, tall and skinny with very curly hair, was wearing pants that were too short, as usual. They never seemed to quite reach his ankles, even when they were new ones.

Marco nodded in Joey's direction – a slow, important nod.

"You're *kidding*," said Joey, almost breathless. "You really did it? You traded that stock on the Internet that you talked about?"

"Yup," said Marco proudly.

"How much did ya make?" Joey asked, eyes growing wide.

"Ten thousand."

"Dollars?"

"No, genius, pennies. Of course dollars!"

"Stand back," said Joey, putting his hand up to his forehead. "I think I'm gonna faint. How much did you start with?"

"You mean in the 'Give Marco a Good Start in Life' fund?"

"Is that really what it's called?"

"Yep. All my relatives have been pitching in since I was born: parents, grandparents, aunts, uncles. After twelve years of birthdays and Christmases, I had about two thousand dollars."

"And you turned it into ten thousand! Awesome! Just awesome" whooped Joey.

"Shhh, keep your voice down." Marco threw a cautious glance over his shoulder. "Do you want the whole world to know? Actually, I also had some money from that summer job two years ago on my uncle's farm in Iowa. So, I'd say, two thousand five hundred dollars to be more exact."

"You used it all? Oh, sweetness!" said Joey.

"That's the sweetest thing I've ever heard."

"Come on, Joey," said Marco. "Keep it quiet."

Marco and Joey's conversation came to an abrupt end when the loudest mouth in the seventh grade descended upon them.

"Hey," said the intruder.

The boy's name was Bart, and his voice was so loud that whenever he talked, people could probably hear him halfway around the world in a remote region of Tibet. He was a big burly kid with a thick neck which, Marco

4

suspected, was built that way to hold up his heavy head, stuffed full of his high opinion of himself.

Though Marco's mother had been a close friend of Bart's mother, going all the way back to their own childhood, just the idea of both families getting together for a picnic one summer caused Marco to suddenly come down with a strange malady rendering him near death's door. His wish to spend any time with Bart was second only to his desire to swallow a handful of live worms, which Joey's cousin, who's in college, told them he had to do for fraternity initiation. Joey and Marco were sure he was making up the stuff about the worms but, hey, you never know.

"Whatta you guys whispering about?" Bart asked curiously.

"Bart, ol' buddy," said Marco, "you'll be among the first to know...when we're ready to tell you."

Bart shrugged and lumbered off.

"We'll talk later," said Marco to Joey as they walked towards the lunch room.

2

...and staring directly at Marco was a child not more than four years old, whose ribs were visible through her thin brown skin.

Problems, Problems, Problems

THE DOORS OF THE SCHOOL CAFETERIA BLASTED OPEN. Reflexively, Marco put up his right arm to block the blow. He didn't really hear the deafening laughter and shouting of the students inside as this was just a typical day in the lunch room of the Benjamin Franklin Middle School. In any event he was too deeply involved in conversation with Joey.

Often, Marco would become so engrossed in an idea or discussion that he would literally loose himself in thought. This was one of those times. He was discussing his recent incredible win in the stock market. If a demolition explosion went off, he would hardly have noticed. Bart and his best buddy, Stu, had sauntered over to the steam tables, quickly surveying the current offerings. Marco and Joey took their places in line.

"Ugh," said Bart as he saw the cheese casserole, bubbling hot and with a crispy golden crust. Then in a voice that could be heard ten yards away he bellowed, "What the hell is that? Looks like someone barfed!"

Mrs. Brown, the lunchroom supervisor, was wearing a dark gray dress with big patch pockets. She was standing behind the counter. Not quite covering the front of the dress was a starched white apron which she now smoothed down with her hands. She looked at the boys and gently shook her head.

"Yeah, tastes that way, too," said Stu, ever ready to second what his friend had just announced.

"I wouldn't eat that even if I were starving," said Bart.

"I wouldn't even give this to my dog," said Stu. "It's gross!"

Marco and Joey just listened as Bart and Stu complained about the day's fare.

Mrs. Brown, who had been taking in the boys' culinary opinions, finally interrupted. "I take it you fellows aren't aware of what thousands of young people are trying to survive on," she said sternly, "how about a handful of rice and a slice of stale bread. I wonder what you'd say if you didn't know where *your* next meal was coming from."

She handed Bart a paper cup with milk. As he started to put it on his tray, he quickly pivoted at the sound of a commotion at the other end of the lunchroom and bumped the tray against the counter. The milk cascaded down to the floor.

"Oh well," he said under his breath, "I'll just get some soda out of the machine." And with that, he meandered away.

"But the milk..." said Stu.

"Just leave it," said Bart.

Marco and Joey looked at each other with raised eyebrows.

"She'll clean it up," said Bart. He nodded towards Mrs. Brown. "That's her job. If she doesn't, she'll get fired. My father's real close to a couple of people on the school board."

Mrs. Brown took a deep breath, and said nothing as she got down on her hands and knees to clean up the spill. Marco and Joey waited good-naturedly in line, as Mrs. Brown seemed to be preoccupied.

When she finished, she wiped her hands on her apron and said, "Do you want the casserole?"

"No, thank you," said Marco. "I guess I'll just have the peanut butter and jelly today."

Joey nodded. "Me, too."

Marco and Joey fixed their sandwiches and grabbed a bunch of raisin cookies while Mrs. Brown waited and watched. Then she put her right hand into her apron pocket and withdrew a letter. Her eyes glanced quickly over the much folded note which seemed to have a partial rip.

Marco studied her and thought he could disern some moisture in her eyes.

"Is everything okay?" he asked.

"Take a look at this," she said to the boys. "It's from my cousin who's traveling with the church's 'Aid to Africa Mission.'"

Marco took the letter, unfolded it gently, and read:

From a distance, it looked like a swarm of black ants descending upon a slightly torn tarp staked with flimsy wooden sticks.

When our bus got closer to the refugee camp, we saw what we already knew. These weren't ants at all, but people, our own, our family, our humanity. There were so many of them; we couldn't even begin to count.

The two food lines seemed impossibly long. The line for water— was forever. Our pastor told us that even the one week we'd spend here would help. Just let everyone at home know what's happening. Please let them know.

Marco returned the letter to Mrs. Brown. She refolded it and put it back in her pocket. Then she took out a creased photo and extended her hand.

The two brown eyes looking out of the photograph were staring directly at Marco. The snapshot was of a child not more than four years old whose ribs were visible through her thin brown skin. She wore nothing above her waist. There was only a torn print skirt covering thelower part of her body.

"Wow," he said softly, his eyes narrowing. "That's the saddest face I've ever seen."

Joey took a quick look, but Marco held on to the photo for a long while.

"Go on," said Mrs. Brown, "you can keep it."

Marco slowly nodded.

She looked at Marco for what was a long moment and then turned to the next student in line.

As he left he called out, "We really do like your cookies, Mrs. Brown."

With their sandwiches in hand, the boys headed toward the crowd that had now collected on the far side of the lunchroom. As they approached the group, Marco noticed his next-door neighbor, and former best friend, Piper, mesmerizing the kids who had gathered.

They *used* to be best friends back when they were in nursery school, but that was before Marco realized it wasn't cool to have a *girl* as a best friend. Now, when they saw each other in the hallways or on the weekends, they just smiled and waved.

He and Joey walked over. Marco noticed Piper's light brown hair, which barely brushed the tops of her shoulders. She was leaning forward. Her wrinkled brows were mostly hidden beneath the full bangs on her forehead. She spied Marco, nodded, and resumed her story.

"...so, Alfred had to actually tie Marta down so she wouldn't get washed overboard," Piper was saying. "Their plan was to reach the Italian shore. When they had first left Albania, they didn't even have an idea what they would be eating in Italy, but they were sure it'd be more than what they were getting at home. Stefania said that Marta and Alfred left Albania after their father died. It was all their mother could do to feed the three younger children. The big meal of the day was only, like, a piece of moldy bread and cheese."

She took a big bite out of her blueberry muffin.

"And just who are these people?" asked Marco.

"They are Stefania's Albanian friends," said Piper. "Stefania is my pen pal."

At first, when their social studies teacher, Ms. Evlin, mentioned the idea of pen pals – connecting with other students around the world via the Internet – the class thought she had lost her mind. But Ms. Elvin was one of those teachers who wanted to creatively engage her students, so on Parents' Night she told the mothers and fathers that she had assigned pen pals to everyone in her class.

Piper put down her muffin and resumed talking to the group. "Now, Alfred and Marta are living in Florence, Italy, but crossing the Adriatic Sea wasn't, like, a lot of laughs."

"Where the hell is the Adriatic Sea?" Joey interrupted. Geography was obviously not his best subject.

"Well, duh," said Piper. "My guess is that it would be somewhere between Albania and Italy."

Actually, when Alfred left Albania he wasn't even sure that he and his sister would make it to dry land. He had heard stories of people drowning, getting caught in treacherous storms and having to turn back, or being picked up by the Italian coast guard and thrown into prison. All the while, Marta and he had to constantly bail the boat with a coffee can as torrents of water splashed in over the sides, threatening to sink the small dingy. The waves were that high.

"One night," said Piper, "there was a huge storm, and their boat almost capsized. Alfred had to take a big chance and tie his sister to the gunwales to keep her from being washed overboard. Finally they landed safely on the rocky Italian coast. They had made it, but Alfred still landed in jail. It didn't seem fair. He was only sixteen."

"The jail part happened after they had been in Italy for a few months. Alfred was working at several part-time jobs, one of which was as a courier for a doctor. He was taking a package from the airport to the doctor's office, which he had done several times before, but this time the doctor wasn't there. He had put his hand on the doorknob and the door just sort of swung open. He looked around and called out, and then walked inside. Since Alfred was just a teenager, and his clothes were kinda crummy, when someone saw him entering the doctor's office, the police were promptly called. The next stop was jail."

Piper finally stopped talking. Her eyes took in the crowd of kids who seemed captivated by her tale.

Marco, doubting the veracity of her story, said, "I take it the Titanic didn't go down. My heart is just breaking. Has somebody got a tissue?" He mockingly rubbed his eyes.

Piper looked up at him.

"Honestly, Marco, it's nothing to joke about. You know, you're a big creep! This is no bull; it actually is a true story, and now this guy's in jail, for crying out loud!"

"Yeah, all right, I see he's got a problem. Hmm... wandering around in a doctor's office when the doctor's not there does sound a tiny bit like breaking and entering to me."

Piper sighed. "Marco, don't you know *anything*? Anyone who looks a little suspicious in Italy seems to get nailed. And if he turns out to be Albanian, he's had it."

"Well," said Marco. "There's a sixteen-year-old kid who enters a doctor's office that should've been locked, and he doesn't look right, so wham! They grab him and throw him in jail. Yeah, come to think of it, they could do that."

"Marco," said Piper, "what do you think? Can you help? Anything you can do? The doctor *did in fact* ask him to go there and he even said it was urgent."

"Jail...jail...jail," Marco repeated, shaking his head. "Well, let me work on that a bit."

Bart had wandered by and overheard the end of the conversation. "So," he said, "great friends you guys have. Any other jailbirds you hang around with?" A moment later he strutted away, sporting a smirk. Stu, eager to add to the torment, sang out, "Tweet, tweet, tweet," and hurried after him.

Bart wasn't watching where he was going and caught his foot in the loosely dangling strap of a backpack that was hanging from the next table.

The backpack belonged to Einstein, whose real name was Albert Stein. Everyone called him Einstein because he wore thick glasses, and his hair stood up on his head, each clump seeking its own direction, almost deliberately. He was also very brainy, so the nickname just stuck.

One time in Math class, Einstein had told his teacher, Mr. Kenilworth, that the correct answer to a problem on the chalkboard was X = 28.7, not 2.87. The teacher looked long and hard at Einstein, not blinking and not smiling. He was even more annoyed when Einstein corrected him a second time, and in the same class period. Each time, Mr. Kenilworth mumbled something under his breath. Reluctantly he made the corrections on the chalkboard.

With his foot trapped in the loop of the strap, Bart's large frame went sprawling. The accompanying thud was followed by a moment of silence and then the gale of giggles coming from the girls' table. A round of applause and cheering from the rest of the crowd filled the cafeteria.

Bart rose, his face beet red. He looked up and saw Einstein, who at that moment was trying to shrink into nonexistence.

"You idiot!" Bart screamed. "Dead meat! Consider yourself dead meat. I'll see you after school, loser. Hope you bring lots of bandages."

"Yeah," said Stu, "you'll need 'em."

When they had left, Einstein cried out, "Oh man, what am I going to do?" His eyes grew big as Marco and Joey joined him at the table. "The big jerk's gonna kill me!"

"Ah, he's all bluff," said Marco. "He'll probably spend the afternoon looking for a dog to kick."

"You think so?" asked Einstein.

The expression on the frail boy's face did not suggest total confidence.

Marco and Joey looked at each other and nodded, but it was clear that neither of them envied Einstein's situation.

Once the three boys finished their lunch, the incident and Bart's threat faded into oblivion. Piper stopped by. "Come up with any ideas yet" she asked. "about getting Marta's brother out of jail?"

"I'm thinking," said Marco. "I'm thinking."

Piper nodded. She knew what Marco could do when he put his brain cells to work.

3

Run, Einstein, Run!

WHEN THE THREE O'CLOCK BELL RANG, THE USUAL STAMPEDE of free-at-last students spilled out of the school building, down the steps and into the sidewalk and street. Marco and Joey pushed open the doors, and there was T-Bone, Marco's dog, waiting as usual. T-Bone had a broad head, anchored by two floppy ears on either side, which were attached to his long thin body.

"He looks like a T-Bone steak, and looks like he needs one as well," stated Marco's Uncle Horace who had given him the puppy. The name just stuck.

T-Bone barked once and trotted over.

"Hey boy," called Marco, "roll over and slap me five."

The dog performed as directed, left paw outstretched. Marco reached into his pocket for a biscuit and tossed it skyward. T-Bone snapped up the treat on the fly and then licked his chops.

"So he's a southpaw," said Joey, walking over. "The mutt's a southpaw. Shakes with his left paw. What a great dog! Give me one of those cookies. Here, T-Bone," he called. "Slap me five."

T-Bone's tail was spinning like a propeller. He walked over to Joey and lifted his left paw. The cookie disappeared into his slobbering mouth. A few minutes later, Einstein joined them.

Joey, continuing his conversation with Marco, said, "So, they just sent it to you in the mail? I don't get it."

"Get what?" asked Einstein.

As the three boys continued on their way home from school, Joey told Einstein how Marco had made a bundle, trading online in the stock market.

"Really?" said Einstein his eyes growing wide. "You bought stock on the Internet? How's that possible?"

"Actually," said Marco, "it was my father's brokerage firm. They sent the letter to me by accident, I guess. The message said, 'Welcome Back.'"

"To you? They sent it to you?"

"Well," said Marco, taking a deep breath, "sort of…in a way. Not exactly to *me*. You see, there was this letter that came addressed to me. My name is Mark P. Blackberry. My father is Mark B. Blackberry. It was probably just a typo."

The letter had come from a brokerage house, where Marco's father bought stocks, sold stocks, and 'took a bath,' as he had said a year ago when the financial markets went south. Marco remembered his parents' heated discussions as his father vowed to stay clear of the markets and stick to his insurance business instead.

Turns out that the brokerage house was less concerned about what had happened and more concerned with getting their old customers to resume trading. "Tomorrow is another day," they wrote in the letter, and so they were offering four months of free trading. The letter had arrived just after Marco came home from camp. He thought it looked cool, and so kept it.

He told his friends, "When I talked to my camp buddy, Jean Louis, about the gold mine that we found, it occurred to me that I might, you know, try trading this stock on the Internet for myself."

"Cool," said Joey. Then, turning to Einstein, he added, "Marco saved every last cent of his birthday money going back to the day he was born – two thousand and five hundred dollars – and our financial wizard here turned it into ten thousand bucks! He actually tripled his money."

"Quadrupled it," corrected Einstein.

"The brokerage house never knew I was a kid," said Marco.

"How'd you do that?" asked Einstein.

"Actually, it was pretty easy! My folks always use the same password for every-thing. Dad says Mom never remembers the password or the pin number for their ATM, but I think he's the one who forgets, so they always use the same one."

"Didn't you feel guilty?" asked Joey.

"Yeah, maybe a little, but not that much. I *did* use my own money. It's not like I stole anything, and I ended up making big bucks, so..."

Nearing the intersection, Marco noticed a group of boys lingering around the empty lot on the other side. It was here that Einstein usually parted ways with Marco and Joey, as the Stein family lived on the west side of town. Bart was waiting just as he said he would, and he had his gang with him.

Marco whispered to Einstein, "Just keep walking. Don't look any of them in the eye. We'll try to distract them."

"Hey guys," Marco said strolling over. "What's happening?"

Bart turned, and as he did, he spotted Einstein out of the corner of his eye, crossing the street.

"There he is!" Bart yelled.

He took off running after Einstein, and his buddies followed close behind.

"Run, Einstein, run!" shouted Marco. "Move those little legs!"

"It's hopeless," said Joey. "Just look at him, Marco."

Einstein sprinted away as quickly as he could, pumping his short legs, his thick glasses sliding down his nose.

"Dead meat," said Joey. "Poor Einstein, he's really going to be dead meat."

4

"...just running – you know, having fun."

The Math Experiment

"WATCH IT, BUDDY! WHERE'S THE FIRE?"

Einstein was running so fast, with his head down, that he didn't even notice, "The Chucker," Benjamin Franklin Middle School's, athletic director and football coach. Players never referred to him by that name, not to his face at least. Direct confrontation called for "Coach Chuckowski," or more often, "Coach Ski."

The Chucker had just left the corner grocery store, package in hand. The collision was head-on, but Einstein was more than 150 pounds lighter than the former Ohio State linebacker, who bounced back. Bart and his gang weren't far behind and they all came to a skidding halt upon seeing the coach.

"So what's going on here, guys?" boomed "The Chucker."

"Coach Ski!" said Bart, breathing heavily and assuming what he thought was his best choirboy look. "We were just having a sort of – a sort of – race."

"Yeah, a race," said Stu.

"That's it," added Hank. "We were running – you know, having fun."

Bart and his "racing friends," were all starters on Benjamin Franklin Middle School's football team. The Chucker frowned at them.

"Racing, my eye!" he said. "I know exactly what you were doing. You guys think you got a position on the team locked down? Cuts are coming up tomorrow, and none of you hotshots have it made yet. You hear me? None of you. Players on my team don't pull this kind of stuff."

Bart tried to explain, but the coach stopped him.

"Knock it off," he said, raising his hand, a gesture that had been known to turn a room filled with mayhem to one of churchly silence in an instant. Bart's mouth snapped shut.

"You," The Chucker said, pointing at Einstein, "what's your name?"

"I'm Albert Stein, sir."

"Tell me what's going on, Albert."

The other boys were looking at the ground, moving nervously from foot to foot.

"Well," said Einstein, his eyes and nose scrunched tight as he looked up and to the left like he was trying to retrieve the answer from some distant place. He knew if he told the coach the truth, he'd only be postponing the inevitable. It might not be today or tomorrow, but Bart's gang would get him sometime.

"We were doing an experiment," he finally announced.

"Yeah, an experiment," said Stu.

"Go on," said the coach.

22

"The question at hand," said Einstein, "is, hmm, if someone, who has shorter legs and is not a very fast runner to begin with, if this person were given a sufficient head start, of say thirty seconds, how long would it take for the other runners, with longer legs, to catch up? Of course, we are talking here about a very short distance. If the faster runners ran twice as fast, it should take them only half as long. So yes, I think the experiment worked."

He turned to Bart, "You boys might have reached me in another ten seconds. Yep, that's about it."

"Albert, what the hell are you talking about?" asked the coach. "These boys looked like they were up to no good. Weren't they chasing you?"

"No, Coach Ski," said Bart.

"Only technically," offered Einstein.

"Yeah," they all agreed, nodding vigorously, "technically."

Turning to the others Einstein said, "Well guys, I guess you helped me prove my hypothesis. Thanks a lot."

"You're sure you're okay?" asked Coach Ski, scratching his head.

Einstein walked away.

"Perfectly sure," he called back.

5

"Bravo Marco!" Stephania wrote. "You are very clever.
I wonder if Piper is right about those other things…"
Marco: "What other things?"

Get- Out- of- Jail- Free Card

THE EMAIL WAS WAITING FOR MARCO WHEN HE ARRIVED home from school. It was from Piper, and it read: *Hey, Marco any ideas about Marta's brother? Being in jail is no picnic you know.*

Yeah, thought Marco, like I'm a magician or something. Abracadabra, poof, he's out! Or, I know, I'll roll the dice and land on the space where I pick up a 'Get- Out- of- Jail- Free' card.

He turned up the volume of his stereo and emailed a reply. At the same time, he leaned back and tried to reach his bookcase to grab the rest of the slice of chocolate cake he had taken from the kitchen.

Two weeks ago, he had attempted the same balancing act, leaning out just a little too far. The ensuing thud sounded as if someone had dropped a wrecking ball right in the middle of his room. The only damage, though, was to Marco's ego and to his arm, both of which were sore for the next few days.

Now, as he leaned back, he remembered. He was a quick learner. This time his extended reach brought its own reward as he popped the cake into his mouth and washed it down with a glass of milk. Then he made a slapping sound with his hands, wiped them on his jeans, and blew the crumbs off the keyboard.

He hunkered back down and began typing, his fingers scurrying around much like the mouse he was directing. He clicked here and there, leaning intently toward the computer as he looked up names, addresses, and phone numbers of people, schools, and hospitals in the United States.

Then he tried to get the same information from search sites in Italy. He even used reverse directories.

At last he keyed in, *Marco Polo Blackberry & Company*, typed in a password, and waited as the website loaded. Last summer, with Einstein's help, he had created the blog, where all of his friends, no matter where they were from, could post pictures, stories and even talk live to each other in the chat room.

Roo, Marco's Australian pen pal, was already in the chat room when Marco logged on. Roo's real name was Rudolph, but the boys at his English boarding school had nicknamed him Roo, which was short for kangaroo, native to Australia.

Hey Marco! Roo typed. *How's it going, mate?*

Roo's home in Australia was on the far side of the world, and he was facing a rising sun as it was early in the morning there. Almost halfway around the globe in the mid-western United States, Marco's fingers were tapping away in the late afternoon. This was a good time for the two of them to talk.

I must to tell ya, Roo continued, *this blog's been busy lately. Joey just posted a message, saying you made a ton of money online. Everyone is dying for more details. Don't hold back on your good buddy. What happened? And how are you going to spend that money?*

Marco smiled and wrote back: *That's for later, Roo. Right now I've got a problem, and I need some info. You mentioned that you had an uncle who was a doctor, right?*

Spot on, answered Roo.

Do you happen to know if all doctors are listed in some kind of medical book? Marco asked. *I mean, is there a book of doctors in different countries?*

Roo explained that his uncle was listed as a member of the Australian Medical Society and the emergency Physicians Association, as well as on the staff of the university medical school. *Took a special assignment with some kind of a hospital ship, too,* Roo wrote. *He's a really cool guy. You'd like him, Marco. So why'd ya need to know all this stuff anyway?*

Marco briefly explained about Marta's brother, Alfred, and the situation in Italy.

Jail? Roo typed in bold. *The guy's in jail? Well good luck. Sounds like you're gonna need it. Talk to you later, gotta go.*

As Roo logged off, Marco noticed that Joey and Einstein were both now online.

Darn, Marco typed to no one in particular. *I don't know why Piper hasn't gotten back to me. I'm doing her a big favor, saving her friend's tail, and she hasn't returned the email I sent her over an hour ago. Can you believe that?*

I take it you're somewhat familiar with that device known as the telephone, typed Einstein. *Mr. Alexander Graham Bell would be very annoyed with you for forgetting such a fine instrument.*

Hey yeah, typed Marco. *I didn't think of that. Got to go.*

✲ ✲ ✲

Piper picked up on the third ring, and recognizing her voice, Marco blurted out,

"Listen now, Piper, this is what I need you to do."

"Marco, is that you?" Piper interrupted. "And what ever happened to 'hello' and 'how's it going?'"

"Right," said Marco. "How are you?" And then, without waiting for a reply, he said, "Look, contact your friend Stefania and get her on 'Marco Polo Blackberry & Company' blog as soon as possible. Can you do that?"

"Hey genius," said Piper, "it's the middle of the night there right now. She lives in Italy, remember? What have you got in mind?"

"I've got a plan," said Marco. "Just make sure Stefania gets online. And you should, too, in case I need an interpreter."

"Very funny," she said. "Seriously, Marco, have you thought of a way to help?"

Just then there was a knock at the door.

"I think I may have found a way to get Alfred out of jail," he said, "but I've gotta run now. I'll be back online at 7:00 tomorrow morning, and I'll talk to you then."

☆ ☆ ☆

For such a little girl, only five, Lilly's knock was surprisingly loud; one would have thought she was locked in the trunk of a car rather than just on the opposite side of the door.

"Come in, Lilly," Marco called out.

She entered.

"Eww," Marco said, holding his nose. "What's that smoky smell? Smells like burned garbage. P.U."

"Very funny," said Lilly. "It's macaroni and cheese, and I made it all by myself. Who were you on the phone with?"

"That, my little sister, is none of your business."

"I bet it was a girl," Lilly said in a cooing voice. Then she glared at him, "Was it? Was it that Piper?"

Marco's ears started to tingle, and his face turned beet red.

"Aha!" she said, jumping up and down with glee. "I was right! It was Piper."

"So what. Big deal. Hey, how come you're in my room in the first place?"

"You did say, 'come in,' you know. And anyway, I'm supposed to tell you that it's time for dinner."

"Well, now you did. And now you can leave. By the way," he called out to her as she started walking out of the room, "What's for dinner?"

"Macaroni and cheese," Lilly said, as she turned and gave him her broadest smile showing all of her teeth; her eyes were dancing.

Bounding down the staircase, he could hear her singing, "Marco has a girlfriend! Marco has a girlfriend!"

✡ ✡ ✡

Promptly at 7:00 AM the next morning, Marco logged on to the blog. Piper and Stefania were already waiting for him.

Stefania, you're there? he typed. *Glad you could make it. You too, Piper, it's important.*

Yup, I'm here, Piper answered.

Si. I mean, yes, Stefania typed back slowly. *I really appreciate much, all you are doing for my friends.*

No problem, wrote Marco. *Listen, Piper told me the whole gruesome story. Now here's what I want you and your friend Marta to do. Go to the building where Marta's brother Alfred went to deliver the package to the doctor. See if you can find a directory in the lobby or entrance hall. You know, some kind of listing of all the offices in that building. I need the doctor's full name. And get the exact spelling. That's important. Then, I want you to plan to hang around the building for an hour or so. Ask some of the people entering the building if they know this doctor. If they work there they might know him or at least know what kind of doctor he is.*

What do you mean by what kind? asked Stefania. *He's a doctor, just a doctor.*

Marco replied: *Stefania, trust me. There are all kinds of doctors. He could even be a dentist.*

I never thought about that, Stefania wrote. *Piper, you were right.* He is *very smart!*

I never said that, typed Piper.

Yes, you did, said Stefania, *in that note you sent to me. You also said some other things, but I won't mention them here.*

You better not, if you want to keep me as a friend, said Piper.

My, you are very sensitive.

Listen, said Marco. *I don't know what you girls are talking about, but if you want my help, let's get on with it. Stefania, how soon can you go?*

The office building is not far from here. Andiamo subito – *I mean, we'll go right away. Ciao, Marco and Piper.*

Yeah, Marco typed. *Ciao, bye, or whatever. Get back to me as soon as you have the information.*

✪ ✪ ✪

At lunchtime, Marco went to the computer lab and opened up his blog. Sure enough, there was a message waiting for him.

The doctor's name is Lorenzo Furlano, Stefania had written just a few minutes earlier. *And he isn't a medical doctor at all, but a biochemist.*

Immediately, Marco went to work on the computer, quickly navigating his way around the Internet. Within fifteen minutes, he had his answer.

Stefania, you still there? Marco typed frantically. *Here's the doctor's address and phone number. If the good doctor's not there, explain the situation to Mrs. Furlano, his wife, and perhaps she'll be able to help you.*

Bravo, Marco! Stefania wrote. *You are very clever. I wonder if Piper is right about those other things she said about you as well. Grazie per tutti. I cannot thank you enough.*

Marco logged off, but before he got up from the desk, he sat alone tapping on the side of his computer. Other things? He thought. What other things?

✼ ✼ ✼

The next day at school, Piper found Marco in the lunch room.

"It took only twenty-four hours and Albert was released!" she announced. "Great job, Marco! Thank you."

"Way to go," said Joey.

"How'd you do it?" asked Cindy, who was sitting next to Piper.

"With my crystal ball!" Marco laughed.

"Come on," said Cindy. "Tell us for real."

"Well," Marco explained, "even though I was given the doctor's name, I still couldn't find him in the phone book because he didn't live in the city. But then I used the most important piece of information of all."

"And that was...?" asked Joey.

"Well, it turns out that the good doctor is not a medical doctor but a doctor with a Ph.D. He's a biochemist, a really famous one. There is only one major university in Florence with a department like that – it's the University of Florence. In fact, the doctor is the head of the Biochemistry Department, entomological Studies. Using the information on the university's website, plus a reverse directory, it didn't take me long. See, they list all the professors at the university and the subjects that they teach along with their phone numbers."

"What's this *entomological* studies?" Cindy asked.

"Insects, you know? Bugs. It turns out that the good doctor knows practically everything there is to know about bugs."

Cindy wrinkled her nose. "Gross," she said. "The only thing you need to know about bugs is how to squash them."

6

Move mountains, jump tall buildings in a single bound.
It's a bird; it's a plane...

Call Me Marco Polo Blackberry

SIX MONTHS EARLIER ON A SATURDAY NIGHT AT 6:25 P.M., Marco's father uttered the traditional lament of husbands all over the world: "Let's go, Margaret. We're already late."

Marco stood at the door as his mother bustled around the kitchen, performing that Saturday night ritual that precedes leaving for a dinner party. She grabbed the yellow flowers that were wrapped and waiting for her on the kitchen table, kissed her son quickly on the cheek, and uttered, "Don't forget to go to bed at ten."

"Mom, you've got to be kidding. Saturday *isn't* a school night."

"Okay, dear. Go to bed when you're tired. Just don't make it too late. Auntie M. is baby-sitting."

"Baby-sitting?" Marco's eyes went wide. "*Excuse me*! Have you lost your mind?"

"No, no," his mother replied. "It's not for you. You *do* have a little sister. I didn't think you wanted to tuck Lilly into bed and read stories to her, or did you?"

You're right about that, thought Marco. Offhand he didn't know which would be greater torment: rolling naked in a bed of poison ivy or taking care of his little sister. He was sure God had put her on this earth as his personal test.

Better to let Auntie M. deal with the babysitting. And besides, Auntie M. was really cool.

She was the only person Marco knew who had been around the world twice … or was it three times? Every time she came back from some magical place – and she was always coming back from one exotic trip or another – she brought something for the children, something wondrous. Once, she'd brought Marco a Russian Kazaks' fur hat from Siberia, then a curved dagger with an Arabic inscription from Morocco, and even a "mate and bombilla" used by "gauchos from Argentina."

For Lilly, she always brought dolls, but not your ordinary, boring dolls. These dolls were exquisitely dressed in their native costumes, from every corner of the world. In truth, the dolls were too fragile to play with, so they sat atop Lilly's bookcase, watching over the bedroom. Lilly would often cradle one of her baby dolls, explaining all about the different grand ladies perched on high. She told her dolls that when she grew up, she would wear fine dresses like these and travel to faraway places.

Marco nodded at his parents. When the front door closed, he returned to his room, slipped on his headphones and plugged in his MP3 player, and hit the play button.

After settling Lilly into bed, Auntie M., whose real name was Minerva, the Roman goddess of wisdom and learning, went looking for Marco. The door was ajar. She knocked and entered. He barely looked up as his fingers darted over the key board.

"Glad you're getting so much use out of your computer," she said.

"Auntie M., this is amazing," said Marco, giving her a quick glance. "Best birthday present ever. Thank you, thank you."

She sat down next to him and started speaking about all the knowledge he could gain from the computer, how he could be connected to the entire world through the Internet. "Why even at your young age, Marco, you can roam the entire planet, all with a few taps on the keyboard."

"Why do you call me Marco?" he asked. "My parents call me Mark. I'm Mark P. Blackberry."

"Oh not so," said Auntie M. "Actually, the name on your birth certificate is Marco Polo Blackberry. I know, because I named you."

"Polo?" Marco said. "So that's what my middle initial stands for. That's cool. How'd you think of it?"

"It's a special name," she said. "It's high time you learned something about the man who first owned it."

She explained that Marco Polo was a very famous explorer who lived about eight hundred years ago at the end of the 13th century, and he traveled what was known as the "The Silk Route." It extended from Europe to China and opened a passageway from the west to the east.

"The people living way back then," said Auntie M., "knew virtually nothing beyond their city limits. So when Marco Polo made these trips, he returned with stories of ancient cities and of strange inhabitants. Most people thought he was hallucinating. He gave descriptions of people wearing silken robes, and he told about all the gold and silver that he saw and of wonderful spices and unusual things to eat."

"Gold and silver, very cool," said Marco, "but I'm not so sure about those silken robes. I can see me now, riding my mountain bike, with my long silken robe getting chewed up in the gears. Unusual things to eat? Hmm, like pizza? Give me double pepperoni with extra cheese."

"Well, my comedian," said Auntie M. "it turns out that they probably didn't have pizza, but the spices used on the pizza or in the sauce came to us via 'The Silk route.' Seriously, Marco, your namesake returned with more than just good tasting stuff; he brought back ideas, and he showed his fellow citizens inventions that were totally unknown. He gave the West a glimpse into a world his people barely knew existed. And that was what I was thinking of when it came to giving you a name. How in the world could a person with the name Marco Polo not be a courageous explorer?

"Now let me ask you something else," she continued, "entirely off the subject. What do you know about deer?"

"Just the usual," said Marco. "You know the Bambi stuff and also that Mom is always complaining that the deer are eating her plants."

"Deer are also creatures of habit. Now, in my opinion, there are 'deer people.' Have you ever heard of 'deer people'?"

"Huh?" said Marco.

"Well, I call them that because there are some people who never want to explore any new concept, never want to travel, never want to know anything beyond their narrow little world-view. Did you know that deer never go more than seven miles from where they were born in their entire life? There are some people like that; people who rarely venture very far from home. So I call these people 'deer people.' *You*, on the other hand, Marco, you are always very curious. You are made for this world. Like Marco Polo, you could be a great adventurer, determined, goal-oriented, but you also need to be courageous."

"I know," said Marco. "Move mountains, jump tall buildings in a single bound. It's a bird, it's a plane, no, it's Marco Polo Blackberry!"

"Steady now, my comic book hero. For your information, there *are* men who can move mountains, and I'm not talking about Superman. They're called engineers. As for flying even faster than a plane, just think about our astronauts, where they've been, and what they've achieved." Auntie M. pointed at Marco's computer. "In a crazy kind of way, this is a special traveling ship, where you are the captain. It's like a space ship, one that can carry you virtually anywhere in the world almost instantly. And *you* can accomplish so much..." Auntie M. half-closed her eyes and said very softly, almost to herself, "So many problems... So many problems that cry out for solutions..."

"What kinds of problems?"

"Well, hunger, for one. Have you ever been extremely hungry?"

"Sure," said Marco, "lots of times."

"I rather doubt that. I mean seriously hungry, *desperately* hungry, so hungry that you could hardly walk or think or do much more than just lie there and stare at nothing; so hungry that your stomach turns into tight painful knots."

She paused for a moment and nodded. Marco looked at her. She told him about the many children around the world, no older than Lilly, who couldn't go to a hospital when they got sick because there were no hospitals, no doctors, no medicine where they lived. There were even children who were maimed, sometimes killed, in skirmishes or wars.

"It makes me so sad," said Auntie M.

"But how can I help? It all seems like a big job, and if adults can't even find an answer..."

"I'm not sure I have that answer, but if you use your imagination you might find a fresh way of seeing things."

Auntie M. paused. She seemed to be looking out, somewhere into the distance.

Then she shook her head and said, "You have a good mind, Marco. Use it. You have to think of things that haven't ever been tried before. You and other young people could make a difference. Just don't become mentally *stuck*," she cautioned.

"Do you remember that fable from India, the one about the blind men and the elephant? I'm sure I read to you when you were little?"

"Yeah, kinda," said Marco, "I remember some of it."

"Well, let's see... " Auntie M. began.

> "There were four blind men who unknowingly were led to a different part of an elephant. 'Each one of you must tell me what you think is before you,' said a man who could see.
>
> The first man was led to the squirming trunk. 'Oh my,' he said. 'This is definitely a very big snake.'
>
> The second was led to one of the tusks. 'No, no,' he said, touching the slick ivory protrusion which was sharp at the end. 'It's a spear,' he announced. 'Most decidedly, a spear.'
>
> The third blind man touched the elephant's ear. 'Why, it's a fan,' he replied.
>
> 'A flopping fan.' The final blind man was led to the tail.
>
> 'You are all wrong,' he said, grabbing hold of the tail. 'A rope!' he proudly decreed. 'Of this I am certain.'

"So," said Auntie M., "the way we look at things, very definitely affects what we believe."

"With those four guys," said Marco, "it was the way they *felt* things."

"Right," said Auntie M. with a smile. "Each of us experiences things from our own perspective, which sometimes can be wrong, incomplete, or just

41

plain different. Learn about the world, Marco; find out for yourself. Be a great adventurer. Just don't be ordinary!"

"Is that why you like to travel, Auntie M.? To get to know people from other places and understand why they think the way they do?"

"It is indeed," she said. "And when I travel, it is so obvious to me that deep down, we're really not all that different; we're very much the same."

Later that night when Marco went to bed, he started wondering. *Not ordinary? Could there be a great adventurer inside of me?* As he drifted off to sleep he made up his mind. *Tomorrow. Yes, he thought, tomorrow. I'll tell Mom and Dad and everybody. From now on call me,* Marco Polo Blackberry.

7

"Fun." The word just hung out there with no place to go.

Camp Misery

Canada

CANADA WELCOMES YOU, BIENVENUE AU CANADA! SAID the large sign in English and French. *Canadian Customs Straight Ahead,* read the smaller one. Marco stared out of the window of the bus, his chin resting on his left hand, and commenced counting the telephone poles on the side of the road. At seventy-four he suddenly felt a thud from the back of his seat. He gritted his teeth as he felt something poking him.

"Hey, cut it out," Marco called while turning around.

The two boys behind him were at each other again as they had been on and off for most of the last hour. They were arguing about comic books, candy, electronic games—about everything.

"That game's mine! You'd better give it back to me," screeched a short, stocky kid who had mentioned earlier that his name was Ted. Marco knew he was wearing his heavy camping boots because he had felt them kicking his seat.

"I like this game," was his seat-mate's rejoinder.

His name was Rick, a tall bony redhead, afflicted with a bad case of acne.

"I think I'll just keep it," the tall redhead said, holding it in his raised hand.

Ted made a huge leap, his blue baseball cap falling off and landing under the seat. He got Rick in a firm choke hold, and the boy's face began to turn red much like his hair. Suddenly, Rick pushed his palm against Ted's chin, forcing his head back.

The inevitable chant of, "fight, fight, fight," erupted from all over the bus.

"Give that back to me or else," Ted shouted, as the tall boy held the game even higher above his head, a big grin plastered all over his face.

"Why don't you come and get it?" Rick teased. "What's the matter, Shorty?"

Ted then lowered his head and made a bull-like lunge at Rick's midsection. The two boys tumbled into the aisle, tightly locked in combat. A few of the other kids from the back of the bus wandered over.

The biggest kid on the bus, a boy wearing a varsity football jacket, took a firm hold of the red-headed boy's arm and yanked the game away from the owner—just because.

As the wrestling continued, the other kids were cheering, or was it jeering? Marco couldn't tell. He turned away and looked out of the window. With a big sigh, he continued counting the telephone poles.

Suddenly, the bus slowed and came to a halt.

While turning his body around, the bus driver shouted, "Knock it off or I'll come back there and throw you guys off the bus! That's right; I'll dump you somewhere in Canada, no money, just the clothes on your back."

Not quite sure if the driver really meant what he said, the assembled crowd decided to take the safe path and ambled back to their seats. Marco noticed that the shorter kid who had been fighting had a cut on his lip. He picked up the blue cap that had fallen off in the scuffle and put it back where it belonged. Marco shook his head and took a deep breath.

A few minutes passed and then the boys in the seat behind him resumed the warfare.

"I get 'Captain of the Universe' first," he heard one of them demand.

Marco's father had described the wonders of a camp experience in the wilderness of Canada, how it was time to learn what poison ivy looks like, to take trips deep into the woods, swim in mountain streams, and sleep under the stars. He talked of mountain climbing, canoeing, hiking, and all sorts of outdoor activities.

He remembered his father saying, "Why, you'll even catch your own fish, which you'll cook yourself at a campfire," his brows would to arch.

"Sounds like *you* want to go, Dad," Marco replied.

That was when his father got that weird expression. He would wrinkle his nose and eyebrows, looking a bit like a pug dog as his eyes became slits. Then taking a very deep breath he would hold it in his cheeks as his face puffed up like an inflated balloon. All at once, the air rushed out of his father's mouth. It was in a great hurry to leave.

After a short pause his father had asked, "Why not just give it a try?" His eyes pleaded. "It's only for four weeks, it's not forever, and it will be a lot of fun."

Fun. The word just hung out there.

Marco returned to his book. Ted, who lost out on the comic book, peered over the edge of the seat, his baseball cap now perched precariously atop of his head.

"Whatcha reading?" he asked Marco.

"Just a book."

"What kind of book?"

"A biography."

"Huh, what's a bi-grafee?"

"It's a story about someone's life," Marco said.

"Whose?"

"A guy named Harry Houdini,"

"Who's Harry Howdy?"

"Not Howdy, Houdini."

"Well, who is he?" the boy asked again.

"He was only probably the greatest magician who ever lived, that's who," said Marco.

"Hey cool," said the stocky kid. "Can I read it?"

"Yeah maybe," Marco said, even though he had no intention of lending his book to that guy.

The intruder sat back in his seat, and Marco went back to reading.

"I've heard about Houdini," said the boy seated next to Marco. "I'm Jean-Louis. Want some Chocolate Chews?"

"Sure," said Marco.

"I'm from Canada," the boy continued. "Where're you from?"

"Little town in Illinois not too far from Chicago. How come you're going to this camp?"

"My parents got divorced this year," said Jean-Louis. "My Mom moved to the United States, and I was just there visiting her. Actually I live with my Dad here in Canada. I had another month of vacation before school but my Dad has to work. He thought camp would be just the thing for me.

"The advertisement said, 'A summer experience to challenge boys physically and mentally, to help boys develop the skills needed to cope in today's world.' I guess I'm in real need of coping skills.' Anyhow, my dad was very impressed with that," he added. "What about you?"

"Yeah, that got to *my* dad, too," said Marco. "I think all fathers want their kids to be like commandos. Anyway, Dad had a friend who'd sent his own son to this camp last summer. He insisted that his kid had had the time of his life. Came back really 'tough.' My father thought *that* was a good idea: ten-mile hikes, rappelling yourself down a rock wall, living in the woods with rattlesnakes and tarantulas. How could any kid resist all that?"

The bus finally stopped and the camp director, Mr. Forge, climbed on board. His T-shirt was glued tightly to his muscular body. He called everyone to attention and gave them a hearty welcome to Camp Thistle Bee. The bullhorn he used grabbed the attention of those even in the back of the bus. His voice was very loud, very commanding, and Marco didn't think, very friendly.

Mr. Forge informed the campers that the tent assignments were tacked to the big tree and that the tents were located down the hill. He pointed to his left. The boys disembarked.

All Marco could see were two large cabins in the clearing. Beyond that was nothing but dense woods. One of the cabins was for the counselors, Marco learned later. It had an attached tiled shower area. The other great cabin served as the dining/meeting room.

"After you stow your gear in your tents, I want all of you to put on your hiking boots," said the camp director, again using his bullhorn.

"At fifteen hundred hours" he bellowed, "you'll assemble back here ready for a little hike. Five miles just to get warmed up."

"Bad news," thought Marco, "this guy's talking military talk; definitely not a good sign."

He glanced at his watch. It was a quarter to three, civilian time. He turned and looked at his new friend, Jean-Louis. They both seemed to be having trouble swallowing.

Marco found his name on the big board tacked to the tree.

"I'm in tent nine," said Jean-Louis.

"Hey cool," said Marco. "We're in the same tent. Maybe our luck's beginning to turn. According to the map, it looks like it's way down there. See, there's an opening in the forest down the slope."

"C'mon," said Jean-Louis, hurrying down the trail.

"Wait a minute," Marco yelled as he ran back to the bus. "I left my book."

When he returned and headed down towards the tents, one of the counselors stood in the pathway, arms folded across his chest.

"Did you hear Mr. Forge tell everyone to go to the tents and return wearing hiking boots?" he asked Marco.

"I heard him," said Marco, "but I left my book on the bus."

"What's your name?" asked the counselor.

"Marco, Marco Blackberry"

"Well, Marco Blackberry, I'm Mr. Garvey. Mr. Garvey, *sir*, to you," he said, pointing to the nametag on his shirt. "A little advice for you, Marco Blackberry: You take real good care of your gear, and we'll get along famously. understand?"

"Yes, sir, Mr. Garvey, sir," Marco repeated.

Then he ran down the trail to where Jean-Louis was waiting.

"What was so important about that book?" Jean-Louis asked.

"It's all about Harry Houdini who was an escape artist and perhaps the world's *greatest* magician. I think I can learn a few things from Mr. Houdini." Then he added in a stage whisper, "About escape!"

As the boys walked quickly to the tented area, they spotted a large sign with rope letters that read, "CAMP THISTLE BEE."

Camp Thistle Bee thought Marco? No way. Make that Camp *Misery*.

8

Hooked

ANOTHER OF CAMP THISTLE BEE'S SINGULAR CHALLENGES was the two-day trip where the campers slept and ate outdoors and caught and prepared all their own food. It was only the second day of camp and Mr. Garvey, everyone's least favorite counselor, stormed into the tent irate about something. Marco had dubbed him, "Igor," because he reminded him of some sadistic assistant of a mad scientist.

Now it was day one of their two-day hike and Igor, hands on hips, chin thrust forward, said to the boys who had assembled next to a swiftly flowing stream, "Well, you creatures of the wilderness, in this particular stream, there reside trout. Many, many trout. Big, fierce fighting trout. If you fail to catch your dinner here, trust me, you're going to be very hungry."

Marco's eyes grew wide as he looked over at Jean-Louis.

"Not to worry, my friend, if there's one thing that we Canadian boys know how to do, it's fish. Let's head upstream a little. We need a quiet spot."

"Right with you, oh 'child of the wilderness,' mighty provider of all things good to eat," joked Marco.

After finding a good spot, both boys baited up with the worms that they had gathered earlier, and cast out into pools some twenty feet apart. Marco quickly realized that worms did not voluntarily stay attached to a hook.

About ten minutes later, he looked over and noticed Jean-Louis, giving his rod a gentle tug, then a real jerk. The rod began to bend and dance as the Canadian boy gently and steadily pulled his fish toward the shore. Then, with a flick, he plucked a foot-long rainbow trout from the stream."

"How many of those things have you caught?" Marco asked.

"That's my third. You?"

"Not even a nibble. Can't keep the damn worm on my hook. What's your secret?"

"Aha! Let a Canadian boy show you how to do it."

Jean-Louis unwound the worm and, with a deft flick, pierced the bait several times with the barbed point.

"Yuck," said Marco. "That's barbaric."

"Not if you want to catch dinner."

Marco sucked in some air, gritted his teeth, and impaled the wiggling worm on his hook.

"That's a start," said Jean-Louis. "Now flick your line right into the middle of that pool in front of you—real gentle-like."

All of a sudden, Marco felt something nuzzling the end of his line. Then he felt a pull that bent his pole almost in two.

"Yow wee," he yelled. "I've got, I've got, I've got... wow, it's huge!"

Jean-Louis's advice seemed to break his losing streak. Now he simply lowered his line and the fish appeared to jump onto the hook.

"Unbelievable," said Marco as he pulled yet another out of the water.

This last one was the biggest by far.

"Come to me, big guy. Come to Papa" he said, cooing to the fish. "You're just what I've been waiting for."

They had each gotten six fish already and Marco was working on taking the hook out of this huge one. He grasped the hook, gingerly taking it out of the fish's mouth, when all of a sudden, the creature leaped up in the air with one last bit of strength. Marco let out a yelp as his finger was impaled on the hook.

"Damn," he mumbled.

Jean-Louis came running. "Oh geez," he said when he saw the wound.

It was bleeding a lot.

"Marco, keep your finger upright," said his friend, kneeling next to him.

He gently moved the hook back and forth, but the thing was clearly determined to stay just where it was.

"I hate to say this," Jean-Louis said, "but this one calls for Igor."

Jean-Louis cut the line so just the hook remained, imbedded in Marco's finger. It took quite a while, but Mr. Garvey knew his stuff. He worked the hook gently back and forth until it came out of it's hiding place under the skin.

Once the hook was out, Marco applied pressure to the wound and dipped it into the icy water of the stream. The throbbing finally began to ease. Mr. Garvey then wrapped his finger with some bandages from the first aid kit.

"Must have been some fish," he said.

"It was," said Marco. "Can't wait to show you the others."

Ted, the stocky kid from the bus, couldn't help calling out, "Hey, Marco, I see a fish caught *you*!"

Marco turned and made a face.

"Let's go back and pick up our dinner," he said to Jean-Louis.

When the boys returned to their spot on the river, all they saw were some bones and scattered fish parts. In the distance they caught a glimpse of a raccoon, his mouth full, and to Marco's eyes, the little thief was actually chuckling.

9

His screams resonated in Marco's ear for what felt like a full five minutes.

Dinosaur's Graveyard

THE WORST DAY FOR MARCO STARTED WHEN ONE OF CAMP Thistle Bee's returning campers, Rick, the tall red-headed boy with acne that had seemed to have just flared up, approached Marco and Jean-Louis.

"I hear you tenderfeet are going to take that hike up Devil's Peak," he said. His grin, Marco thought, was not exactly reassuring. "See you up there and good luck. You'll need it," was his parting shot.

It wasn't so much the climb as the crossing of the ravine that topped the list of horrors at Camp Thistle Bee.

The campers had stopped at the edge of the deep gorge. Marco looked down at a ribbon of water far below. A very long and very wide log was lying across the ravine. It was split in half, its ends resting on either side. The log was relatively flat on its upward side, but that did nothing to slow Marco's heartbeat.

Down below, the white water was rushing through the narrow passageway, churning along the river bed, sending spray far into the air.

"How wide do you think the river is here?" Marco asked Jean-Louis.

His friend shrugged and said, "Well, it's not the wide Missouri, but it'll do."

Marco looked at the net strung about six feet below and nodded.

"They're really looking out for us," he muttered.

One by one each boy was fitted with a protective rope strapped around his waist and chest. With a slight nudge and a cry of "Nothing to it, camper," the victim made his way across the gorge.

Rick, the veteran, meandered across easily, oblivious to the dangers.

Guy looks like he's taking a walk in the park, Marco thought.

The camper who went just before Marco was visibly trembling. At the midpoint of the crossing, he violated the cardinal rule of climbers; he looked down. His foot slipped, and he tumbled over the edge.

His screams resonated in Marco's ears for what felt like a full five minutes. The boy landed in the net unscathed, yet even as the counselors were pulling him out, he wouldn't stop screaming.

"Move up, Marco," said Igor.

Igor and another counselor secured the ropes tightly around Marco as they had with the other boys. There was an aluminum D-shaped ring that had a snap link, called a carabineer, standard gear for rock climbing. Igor clipped it to a rope around Marco's waist which was attached to the spotter on the bank.

As he approached the edge of the ravine, Marco kicked a small rock over the edge. He waited for the sound of the rock hitting bottom. What seemed like a full ten minutes later, Marco heard the faint "kerplunk."

"Let's go," yelled Igor.

Marco froze for a moment. He couldn't get the other boy's screams out of his mind. Very slowly he stepped carefully onto the log.

"Nice and easy," he said under his breath. "Slow steps, teeny tiny steps, teeny tiny steps."

"Don't think about what just happened," said Igor. "You're doing just fine."

With that sage advice, Marco tried not to think about what just happened. Then the "pink elephant" game popped into his head, just like those times when he was walking home from school and someone would say, "Bet you can't stop thinking about enormous pink elephants."

And sure enough, visions of enormous pink elephants would fill Marco's head. There were pink elephants dancing, pink elephants singing, even big pink elephants riding little baby tricycles. Marco smiled. Suddenly and surprisingly, Marco found himself on the other side of the ravine. The other boys began to clap, all of them, that is, except Rick, the veteran hotshot who had heard Marco mumbling when he first stepped onto the log.

Rick began to mimic Marco's mantra, "Teeny tiny, teeny tiny."

Naturally, the other campers began to chime in until the chant became a crescendo, echoing down the ravine.

Marco, so labeled, was stuck with the title, "Teeny Tiny" for the rest of the day.

When the campers assembled on the other side of the ravine, they hiked on down to the Dinosaur's Graveyard where they plucked baloney sandwiches from their backpacks. Dinosaur's Graveyard was actually an open gravel pit, long abandoned. A few summers ago, some of the campers found a few large bones that one of the counselors said were probably femurs, or the thighbones of large animals. Not about to settle for "large animals," the boys announced the bones were clearly those of very large, very prehistoric creatures, and thus the gravel pit become Dinosaur's Graveyard.

Marco moved off by himself to eat his sandwich, having had enough of the "teeny tiny steps" chant. Jean-Louis came over and sat beside him. They ate quickly and then Marco pointed to the path at the edge of the gravel pit.

"What do you say we do a little exploring?"

Jean-Louis leapt to his feet. "Lead on, Marco Polo Blackberry."

The path curved up the hill and around the back of the mountain.

"Do you think there really were dinosaurs here thousands of years ago?" Jean-Louis asked.

"Could be," said Marco, "but I doubt those other kids found dinosaur bones – a large cow or maybe a buffalo."

"Yeah, maybe a horse," added Jean-Louis. "If I were home, I could look it up on the Internet. I could find out all about different kinds of dinosaurs, buffalos, and horse bones. I'm very good on the computer. Do you have one?"

"I sure do. I got one from my Auntie M. as a birthday present. Once I got the hang of it, it was smooth sailing. I kept finding all kinds of weird and cool things. Hey, I've got an idea. Let's email each other after camp."

"Deal," said Jean-Louis.

They had been walking for quite a while, oblivious to the passing time, when suddenly Jean-Louis stopped and pointed in the direction of heavy growth in the nearby woods.

"Marco," he whispered, "I don't want to alarm you or anything, but over there at the edge of the woods is a bear, a very *large* bear. And he seems very interested in *us*."

The boys froze, trying hard not to breathe. Abruptly, the bear turned and strolled off in the opposite direction. The two boys very quietly, very slowly, backed away, making sure to keep the beast in view. Then quite suddenly, the bear seemed to vanish into the forest.

Out of the corner of his eye, Marco noticed the entrance of a cave and motioned for Jean-Louis to follow.

"Let's wait here for a bit to be sure he's really gone," said Marco.

Though the cave was dark, it wasn't too long before their eyes began to discern the general shape and the craggy sides.

"This cave's huge," said Jean-Louis.

"It's big, all right," Marco said, "but I'm not dead sure it's a cave at all. Seems more like an old mine or something."

"You know," said Jean-Louis, "if I were a bear, I'd think this place would be a great place to make a home."

"Maybe," said Marco, "but the bear we saw seemed to be heading in the opposite direction."

"Well, there's nothing here," said Jean-Louis. "This is neat. You could actually hide out here for some time."

After a while, the boys emerged from the cave, thankful there was no sign of any bears.

"I think we'd better head back," Marco said.

Jean-Louis nodded. But when they returned to the Dinosaur's Graveyard, not a soul was in sight.

"What are we going to do?" asked Jean-Louis.

"They can't be that far away. We better make up some time. Let's see, I think the camp is south of here, isn't it?"

"Yes, but we don't have a compass. I hope we're not going to have trouble finding our way back."

"Don't you remember what the counselor told us about moss always growing on the north side of trees?" said Marco.

Jean-Louis nodded.

"Look. Moss," said Marco, pointing to a big spruce. "So south ought to be... that way." He pointed in the opposite direction. "We'll walk south until we find the main road."

A half hour later, the boys broke into wide smiles when they came to the main road.

"Guess we got lucky," Marco said.

It was then that the boys learned how fleeting luck can be. When they finally arrived at camp, there in front of the mess hall was a very big, official-looking Suv and two uniformed men on horseback. The red light on top of the green van was blinking on and off. On the side, they could see the words printed in large black letters, "Royal Canadian Mounted Police."

Mr. Forge was standing beside the car with the ranking Mounty. His arms were folded. He was not smiling.

"Where in God's name have you two been?" he asked.

Both boys, heads bowed, mumbled something about a bear and a cave and then went silent.

"A bear, was it?" said Mr. Forge. "Well, boys, you now have a job awaiting you. If you're diligent, you should be finished in, oh, three days maybe?"

The entire next day, Marco and Jean-Louis were on their hands and knees, scrubbing the counselor's bathrooms and showers.

Marco took a final swipe at the floor, stood up ready to join the human race once again, when Igor entered. True to his name, he handed them a box of cotton-tipped swabs.

"Good job, guys," he said. "Now let's see what you can do with the grout between the tiles."

Definitely, Marco thought. He's the sadistic assistant to a mad scientist.

After Igor left, Marco turned to Jean-Louis. "I'm not putting up with this anymore. I'm going to do something. I've had about enough of Camp Misery!"

"Me too," said his friend, "but what do you have in mind?"

Marco looked once around the shower stalls to make doubly sure no one was there, and then whispered, *"Escape..."*

10

Marco: "Don't you remember what the bad guys had in mind for those kids?"
He ran his fingers across his throat.

The Great Escape

PEERING AT THE CALENDAR POSTED IN THE MESS TENT, Marco noted that in three days, the night sky would show no moon. Though he didn't think Houdini's tricks would work in these circumstances, a pitch black night was just what he craved.

Jean-Louis was as eager as Marco to make the great escape.

"Listen," he said, "I've got an idea. We can leave camp heading north and then go due west towards the town of Jakely. I know all about that place 'cause it's only ten miles from my Dad's ranch. Some of the kids from my school live in the area nearby. Maybe they could hide us until camp ends."

For the next two days, Marco stashed extra food in his knapsack. He grabbed some hard cheese that was in individual wrappers, snuck some mini boxes of cereals that were always put out for breakfast, along with a few apples and some bananas and a few cookies. Then he took extra sandwiches which he hid under his sweatshirt until he could get back to the tent and tuck them into his sack. Jean-Louis did likewise.

When the camp canteen opened that afternoon, the boys bought small bags of pretzels and those *really* important staples: Foot-Snappers and Gooey Squirts.

Marco especially liked the Foot-Snappers. They were in the shape of a foot and had caramel inside which, when the candy coating melted, the caramel would stick to the roof of his mouth. He would then walk around the house making a snapping noise with his tongue. It drove his mother crazy, which, for Marco, was one of the extra benefits.

And so the night came, the one Marco and Jean-Louis had been waiting for. The sky was very dark because there was no moon, but the endless array of stars sparkled bright and clear. It would be hard to check for moss in the blackness of the night, but Marco knew a lot about the constellations. The Milky Way would give up its secrets if one knew where to look, and Marco knew.

With just a glance up at the evening sky, he could find the Big Dipper. The two stars that formed the side of the cup always pointed to the North Star. This was also the beginning of the handle of the Little Dipper. Once you knew where north was, you could find any direction.

"Jean-Louis," cautioned Marco. "I think we will be as good as dead before we even start if we let any campers know what we're up to. We'd better be careful and not say anything."

"Right on!" said Jean-Louis as he looked over at Marco. "There's always one creep that has to tell an adult. So we'll go tonight then, right?"

"You bet," said Marco, giving him a 'thumbs up.'

By ten o'clock, the tent was filled with snoring and heavy breathing. Marco and Jean-Louis crept out from under the flap. They wore hiking boots and strapped on their knapsacks which were stuffed with the essentials. Marco gripped his Dorby-Halogen-Strobe flashlight tightly in his hand. Rubbing it he smiled as he remembered the time he went with his mother to pick out his camping supplies. She had finally given in to his pleas and suggestions. His Super Duper-Dorby-Halogen-Strobe flashlight was priced at three times that of all the other flashlights on the rack.

"But Mom," he had said, "I've been reading about what creatures live in the Canadian woods. There's this one snake that's about seven feet long. Then there's a smaller one whose bite can kill a fully grown buffalo in thirty seconds." Just to drive home his point, he added, "Another type comes from miles around to one location and slithers together with the others, packing themselves into dens, as many as twenty thousand at a time. Then there are the dangerous and deadly rattlesnakes."

Yes, he had told her all he knew about snakes, but he realized that it was the big crawly insects that finally did the trick. A son learns to know a mother, and Marco was well aware she hated big slow moving insects. She had no love for the fast ones, either. He had glanced up at her face, and at that very moment, he knew: the Super Duper-Dorby-Halogen-Strobe flashlight was his.

That night, the two boys left their tent creeping under the flap and quietly walked deep into the woods, as they had many times before on various hiking trips— trips made in bright daylight. In the dark, their pace was much more measured and cautious. Once they reached the valley below, the night sky was very visible. The North Star seemed to be twinkling at them, beckoning them, as they found the road they wanted and headed north.

About two hours later, they had arrived. There it was, The Dinosaur's Graveyard, just as they knew it would be.

"Hey, let's climb around the back of that hill and try to find the cave," said Jean-Louis. "It would be a good place to sleep tonight. If we leave early in the morning, we might be able to make it to Jakely by sundown."

After a while, the boys found the mine opening and entered the dark cave. Using his Dorby flashlight, Marco led the way deep inside. They walked around a gently curved barrier which turned out to be a large natural protrusion in the rock wall, a good place to curl up and sleep.

It wasn't very long before Marco said, "Hey, you know what? I'm hungry."

"Me, too. Want a peanut butter and jelly sandwich?"

Marco nodded and stuffed the sandwich down his mouth.

Then he said, "I think I'll have another half. Want to share? And three of those chocolate chip cookies would taste real good."

"We've got to be careful not to use up all our supplies on the first night out," cautioned Jean-Louis.

"There are only three cookies for each of us."

"Hmm," said Marco, "you're right. Well, just give me two."

Then they went outside to gather some leaves to bed down for the night. When they were returning to the cave entrance, the boys heard voices somewhere in the darkness outside. They turned off their flashlights and tiptoed back to what was now their hiding place behind the rock wall.

Three men walked in, engrossed in conversation. They, too, had flashlights. One had a military spotlight, which illuminated the entire cave.

The boys froze.

"Over here," said one of the men. He took a toothpick out of his mouth and pointed. "We went down about 800 meters to pull up a core. There was a place at the 200-meter mark where we were averaging close to 1.5 ounces of gold."

One of the other men whistled softly.

"The big question is the *grade* of the gold," said the third man, "and does this vein continue for any real length?"

"There are two more studies being done," said the first. "I should have the results by the end of summer. My man in Manitoba said the preliminary data on the ore suggested this was the finest quality he had ever seen."

"Hell! This is going to be big, *really* big," said the second man. "I've got my lawyer coming to Jakely tomorrow, and then we're going to buy this Alex K. Mine."

"Or steal it," the first man said. They both laughed.

From their hiding place in the dark, Jean-Louis grabbed Marco's arm and squeezed hard. Marco looked over and nodded, his heart racing as he crouched down even further, pulling himself into a tight little ball.

"Hey, I don't want to get mixed up in any stealing," said the third man. "I don't plan to spend my life in jail."

"Quit your whining. There's nothing really illegal about this. The Alex K.'s been abandoned since the 1970s and chances are we can pick it up for a song and then..."

As his voice trailed off, a satisfied smirk appeared.

"Gold prices are depressed right now," declared one of the other men.

"Yeah, but not for long," said the first, laughing. "I know a guy who's a trader in the commodity markets.

He tells me he thinks gold prices will soon be heading up *big time*. Pago Global!" his voice boomed. "You'll be hearing a lot about that name."

Grinning, he put the toothpick back in his mouth. It was another half hour before the men left. The boys waited. The silence the men left behind was deafening.

"Hey, Marco," whispered Jean-Louis. "You think they're gone?"

"Yeah, they're gone," said Marco.

"I tell you, those guys gave me the creeps," said Jean-Louis.

"I know what you mean. I saw this old cowboy movie once where the bad guys caught these kids they thought had over—heard their plot to steal some cattle. They took them to this cave, tied them up, and gagged them. They wouldn't even listen when the kids said they didn't hear anything, and even if they did, they promised they wouldn't tell."

"Oh yeah, I saw that, too," said Jean-Louis. "Then the dog, the black and white dog, the one that one of the kid's parents said he couldn't keep, came and found them."

"What a great dog! Boy, I loved that movie. Saw it twice."

"Don't you remember," said Marco leaning closer to Jean-Louis. "You know, what the bad guys had in mind for those kids?" He ran his finger across his throat.

Just then Jean-Louis said, "Shhh." And very softly, "Did you hear that?

While holding their breath, the boys could hear a low soft whining. Marco turned on his flashlight and caught sight of a small black bear cub curled up in the other corner.

"Hey, that's cute. And look over here," said Marco, pointing the beam of his light slightly to the left. "There's another little guy."

"Marco," said Jean-Louis, suddenly dropping his voice to a whisper, "I know about bear cubs; they're never far from mama, and there's nothing more dangerous than a mother bear who thinks her cubs are threatened."

Without hesitation, the boys picked up their stuff and edged out of the cave.

"Do you have this feeling something's watching us?" Marco whispered. "Something very big, very black, and very ferocious?"

They didn't wait to see if he was right. They ran as fast as they could in the dark. Marco stumbled on a tree root and skinned his knee. He got up as quickly as he could, saying, "Let's go, Jean-Louis, I'm okay."

They continued running and eventually made their way down to the Dinosaur's Graveyard.

Marco brushed off his pants and noticed a tear at the knee. The few drops of blood had already dried. While huffing and puffing, he turned to his friend and said, "You know something? Three more days cleaning counselors' bathrooms and showers might not be so bad after all."

"You better believe it," added Jean-Louis.

✲ ✲ ✲

It was still dark when the boys arrived at camp, the North Star behind them all the way. To their amazement, no one knew that they had even gone. They both crept under one of the flaps of the tent and crawled onto their cots. Marco pulled his blanket tightly over his shoulders and snuggled under.

It seemed like he had barely fallen asleep when the shrill bleating of the morning bugle sounded. He sat up quickly and took a deep breath. "Damn," he said to himself.

"Another day at Camp Misery!"

11

Lilly: "*I didn't think Mom and Dad looked to thrilled when I told them you were doing serious things on your computer.*"

Filled

Illinois, USA

WHEN IS IT GOING TO HAPPEN? MARCO TYPED OUT.

He was on the computer Sunday morning with Jean-Louis. The boys had been messaging back and forth almost every day since returning from camp.

Listen Marco, came Jean-Louis's reply. *I was in town yesterday – you know, Jakely – and I noticed those guys, the ones we saw in the cave. I overheard them talking. They're filing the papers on Tuesday. Tuesday is the day! Remember we heard them say it was going to be a big strike, that the mine had a very rich vein? Well, it isn't only the vein that's rich, but the entire core is incredibly valuable. There's a lot of gold in that mine, Marco, and when the news comes out, the stock is going to go sky high. The company's called Pago Global. Remember that name; it'll be in the news for sure.*

You're positive, Jean-Louis? Marco replied. *The symbol is* **TSE: pgog** *on the Toronto Stock Exchange?*

I have to enter the exact symbol on my online stock trading account to buy the stock.

Absolutely sure, he said. *You're really going to do it— buy the stock? You're just a kid, you know, and two-thousand five-hundred bucks is all the money you have in the whole world, right?*

Yeah, but deep down, answered Marco, *I really, honestly, positively think this is gonna work. I just feel good about it, ya know what I mean? If I do hit it big, I'm gonna… Nah, that's for later. Right now, I have to concentrate on tomorrow. Sure wish I had a few more days of vacation.*

How are you gonna pull this off?

I'll put my order in at a limit price Monday morning before I leave for school.

What's that thing-— limit price?

Means at a specific price, a certain amount of money per share of stock and only that amount. I learned that from watching my Dad. He used to say, 'Always use a limit order. That's the right way to trade.'

But how do know what price to ask for? asked Jean-Louis.

Oh, I'll just use the price it closed at on Friday, the last time it traded.

Well, good luck. You've got a lot of guts. Try to log on at school. I'll leave you a message if anything changes.

Okay, Marco tapped. *And thanks.*

"Marco, Marco," called Lilly, knocking on his bedroom door. "Mom wants you downstairs. She told me to get you. You haven't finished raking the leaves yet."

"Get lost," said Marco. "I'm busy. Go away! Don't you see that sign?"

"I see it," she said, "but I can't read it. You know that I can't read yet. When I'm six, I'll be able to read your dumb ol' signs."

Though Lilly had just started kindergarten, she didn't take any guff from her older brother.

Marco opened the door. There stood Lilly, her blond hair tied in two long braids, pink ribbons dangling. She placed her hands firmly on her hips just the way her mother did when she was in no mood for back talk.

"Look," he said to her pointing to the sign. KEEP OUT! This word means, 'keep,' and this word means, 'out.' Now here's another sign."

He attached the new sign with tape, just under the original one.

"See," he said, "ESPECIALLY SISTERS. I wrote this one especially for you."

"Okay for you, Marco," she said. "I could really help you. I could be your helper, but not now. You'll be sorry."

Lilly went downstairs to the kitchen. Another five-year-old might have been in tears at that point, but Lilly was dry-eyed. Actually, she had long since held a jaded view of boys, at least the ones in her school where her pigtails had been absolutely irresistible; and there were some boys who couldn't refuse giving a good pull.

Once she found a whole bunch of grasshoppers near the swings and put them right down the back of Bobby Jones' T-shirt. He was the worst pigtail puller in the class.

When he went to the teacher with tears streaming down his face, Lilly got all the kids to sing out "cry baby, cry baby, stick your head in gooey gravy."

The boys no longer found pulling her pigtails compelling.

"Mom, what does 'specially' mean?" asked Lilly as she climbed onto one of the tall kitchen stools near the counter.

"Well," said her mother. "'Special' means unusual and exceptional, and 'specially' is most unusual and most exceptional."

"Am I specially?" asked Lilly. "A specially sister?"

"Well, I think you're special. You're *my* special girl."

"So that's a good thing?" inquired Lilly.

"Indeed it is," said her mother shoving a plate of newly baked cookies towards her. "Taste one of these. They're yummy."

"Well, I don't know," said Lilly, while munching. "It didn't sound so good to me when Marco said it."

☆ ☆ ☆

Marco had ignored all the traditional formalities of arriving home after school on Monday, the usual "Hi Mom, Hey T-Bone" rituals, and raced to his room and onto his computer. He had logged onto the brokerage website and went into his account, or rather, his father's account. He hesitated briefly, tapping the side of his computer.

Well, he thought, they *did* send the letter to *me*, asking *me* to trade stocks and offering four months free, right? Damn right they did!

Still, he tapped.

Marco didn't know how much this trading stuff cost, but he knew it must be expensive. His father was always grumbling about high-priced commissions. He did know this much: commissions were the costs, the money that a customer had to pay every time he bought or sold a stock when he was trading in the stock market. And now, for four glorious, wonderful, fantastic months, these commissions were *free*.

He thought it was probably some kind of come-on, but he also knew that his father swore he would never trade again. If his father weren't taking advantage of free commissions, taking advantage of the offer himself couldn't be such a bad thing.

It's not my fault that they used the middle initial *P* instead of *B*. P, for Polo. That is *me*. So go for it, you 'courageous explorer,' you.

He had placed the trade before going to school in the morning and now staring intently at his monitor, he saw the word, FILLED, in big bold letters in his brokerage account.

"Yes! Yes!" Marco hollered from his room. He had gotten his trade and at his price- 25 cents a share. He'd bought 10,000 shares, using up every last penny of his savings. They had filled his order. He began to tap the side of his computer again.

"Yes, yes what?" asked Lilly as Marco came out into the hallway.

"Yes, yes, my wonderful little sister, *yes!*"

Lilly looked at her older brother, now totally convinced he had finally lost what was left of his mind.

"So what's happening?" asked Lilly. "How come you yelled out?"

"Yelled? Who yelled? I may have said something, but I certainly did not yell."

"Well, I heard you, and it sounded like a yell to me. What's going on?"

As calmly as he could, Marco said, "Nothing. It's nothing, but you can ask me tomorrow."

"Okay," said Lilly, "I will."

Then with a strong voice she added, while lookin up to the ceiling, "I wonder if Mom knows about this?"

But Marco was already down the stairs and out the door.

✲ ✲ ✲

Tuesday after school, Marco again raced home. Up the stairs he went, two at a time, then slammed the door to his room. The door shut so hard that the KEEP OUT sign fell to the floor.

After opening his computer, he logged on to look at his brokerage account. Nothing, no change. He found the website of the Toronto Stock exchange where he could check the price of his stock, "**Tse: pgog**," Pago Global. The opening price was 25 cents; the low price of the day, 23 cents; the high price, 26 cents. It closed, or ended, the day at 25 cents, the same price as yesterday when he bought it. Images of a bright red four-wheel all-terrain vehicle began to fade.

What gives? thought Marco. The news about the gold found in this mine was supposed to come out today, Tuesday.

He checked his email. Nothing from Jean-Louis. Marco tried to contact Jean-Louis, marking his message *urgent*.

Every half hour all evening long he checked. No response.

That night at dinner, Marco hopped up and raced out of the dining room three times before dessert. His mother and father looked at each other. Lilly knew that look.

"He's doing something very important on his computer," she said.

Her mother looked over at her father.

"Humph," was the only utterance coming out of her father's mouth.

After dinner, Lilly said, "You know, Marco, I don't think Mom and Dad looked too thrilled when I told them you were doing serious things on your computer."

"Why'd you say that? You shouldn't have told them anything," he snapped. "It's not any of your business. I don't need you assisting me."

"Oh, yes you do. If I were your helper, I could help you," said Lilly.

"How could you help me?" asked Marco, sighing.

"For starts," she said, "I wouldn't tell on you."

✶ ✶ ✶

Wednesday came. Still no word from Jean-Louis. Maybe he had an accident, Marco thought, or maybe some sneaky kid stole his computer. Oh, hell, maybe he was kidnapped.

Then he remembered Jean-Louis telling him about a coyote that came into town looking for food. He said they do that sometimes when they're sick. The mayor of the town worried that the coyote had rabies and had called in the Canadian royal Mounted Police. They shot the animal dead, right there in the middle of the street.

"Good thing too," Jean-Louis said, "'cause he *was* rabid and that's a terrible way to die."

"This rabies stuff," Marco had asked his friend, "it can kill you?"

"Not *can*," Jean Louis had replied, "but *will*, unless they catch the creature right away. You might survive then, but they'd have to stick this enormous hypodermic needle right into your belly. Trust me: you don't want to get rabies."

Cool it, Marco thought to himself. You're gonna drive yourself crazy. The possibilities swirled through his brain as he went to his room, hesitantly turned to his computer, and logged on. He tapped on the side until the monitor came to life.

And there they were: three emails waiting, all from Jean-Louis!

Marco drew a deep breath and opened the first one.

Jean-Louis explained how the power went out throughout all of southwestern Canada due to an overload of the system. He couldn't email anyone the entire time, but neither could Pago Global.

The second email was short; it merely said: *Did you see the price of the stock?* It was signed: *Your buddy in crime, JL.*

The third said: *Don't sell yet! It's going higher. Everyone in town's talking about it. They say it's the biggest strike in years.*

Marco's first attempt to log onto the brokerage website ended up as it always did when he tried to rush the process. His second attempt was accurate. "Oh my God," he said aloud.

Right on the big black computer screen was the lettering, "PAGO GLOBAL, closed at 50 cents."

Marco couldn't believe it. His stock had doubled.

✵ ✵ ✵

Marco's trip home on Thursday was made at a full gallop—with Joey in tow this time. Marco had told his friend at lunch what his stock had done.

"Pleeease," Joey begged his Mom. "I really need to go to Marco's house after school. And yes," he assured her, "we'll be doing homework. We're working on a school project together."

The project part was true; they *were* working on a history project, but delving into the complexities of a medieval castle was not what either of the two boys had in mind.

"You boys want some snacks?" called Marco's mother, as they ran up the stairs.

"Love some, Mrs. Blackberry," said Joey.

"Me, too," said Marco before slamming the door.

"I'll bring up the snacks," offered Lilly.

"Why Lilly, how very thoughtful of you," said her Mother.

The sign hanging on Marco's bedroom door couldn't be missed. Joey stopped and stared at it.

"What's that about?" he asked.

The original sign had been amended. Under the words, KEEP OUT, ESPECIALLY SISTERS, was an attachment: EXCEPT FOR SISTER HELPERS. Marco assured him it was absolutely, positively necessary. Lilly had found a way to be an indispensable helper.

"Helper? How can she help?" Joey asked.

"Well, her job's to keep Mom away from my room when I'm on the computer, but her most important job is *not to tell*."

✻ ✻ ✻

When the price of Pago Global popped into view, Joey let out a "whoop!"

"Keep it down," said Marco, but he too felt the urge to do a little whooping. After all, it was Thursday, and Pago Global had closed that day at 70 cents. As soon as he could stop his fingers from shaking, he instant messaged Jean-Louis.

How long will this last? asked Marco.

I'm not sure, Jean-Louis wrote back. *I've heard talk of $1.10.*

80

"Hey, why not go for $1.20?" said Joey. "It's got a nice ring to it."

Marco began tapping on the side of his computer. Then he logged off. "Tomorrow," he said to Joey.

"Tomorrow? Tomorrow what?"

"I'll decide tomorrow."

✪ ✪ ✪

Before leaving for school on Friday, Marco sat down and stared at the computer screen. He thought about many things – a snow board, a four wheeled all- terrain vehicle, and a huge flat screen TV for his own room. Then suddenly he had this image of his Auntie M. He could see her, dangling earrings, bright red lipstick, flowing robes and all, and he could hear her, as clearly as if she had been in the room.

"Don't try to take everything for yourself, Marco," she would say. "Try not to be greedy. That's a lousy way to live. If you pick some berries on the road side, leave a little something for the birds." Then, peering over her glasses, she would wink, adding, "The birds will love you for it."

Okay, Auntie M, Marco thought. *Let's see. How about an order to sell at...*

He ran some figures through his mind: $1.10, $1.20. Then, aloud, said, "One buck, that's it. I'm leaving something for the birds."

Though the stock market wasn't opened yet, he entered a limit order to sell all his shares at one dollar. That was the price he wanted, and that was the price he got.

PART II

12

Hakim: "…there's a big world out there." He had seen a glimpse of it – on the Internet.

An Internet Cafe

Africa

IT WAS NIGHTTIME IN JONTU AND A STEADY DOWNPOUR obliterated the moon. Hakim was staring out the window of his two-room mud hut, while listening to the rain clattering on the hard ground. It wasn't a real window, just a small opening on the side, but Hakim could peer out.

If it rained all night, he wondered, would there still be more water in the sky? Would it continue the next day?"

Every year, the monsoons brought rain, day after day. It seemed unrelenting. While occasionally the sun broke through the gray bulging clouds, the large thunderheads would only gather again and finally unleash their contents. Looking down at his two younger brothers as they slept on a straw mat, Hakim studied the outlines their small thin bodies made under the blanket. He gently pulled at the twisted layer so that it covered their shoulders.

All of a sudden something caught his eye.

"Ah ha," he said. "I see you."

Crouching down, he watched as two small light brown bugs crawled toward the sleeping mat and then stopped. The insects looked unusual; they had a glossy yellow sheen coating their hard crusty shells. Clearly they had a mind of their own. Slowly and deliberately the insects moved again. Hakim scooped them up in his hand and gently flicked them out of the window. It was the season of the bugs.

His youngest brother turned, kicking the cover to one side. Hakim drew close and, with a sigh, pulled the threadbare blanket back up again. He was aware now of the pangs he felt in his half-empty stomach. He looked down again at the sleeping mat. In a short while, he too would crawl under that same blanket and draw close to his brothers for warmth.

Tomorrow, he thought, smiling to himself. Tomorrow I'll be going to Port Dannin.

The eighteen kilometer walk to the town didn't worry Hakim. He could easily handle that distance. The trip back, however, would be harder – carrying a heavy bag of corn seeds was a lot of work. The last time he had made the trip, he'd been with his father. At the harbor, the two of them had stood side by side for a very long while, silently watching the big ships at the dock, so wonderful and inviting, strong and stately. How proud they looked in their berths.

"Come away with me, young sailor," they seemed to say.

Stretching his arms wide, Hakim yawned and then turned to join his brothers under the torn blanket.

✿ ✿ ✿

It was still dark when he awoke. His parents were already up, his mother tending the fire in the wood stove, his father sipping weak tea. The man looked up and nodded toward the large bag lying by the door. He told Hakim to fill it all the way if he could.

"These should pay for an entire sack, Hakim, if the price of corn seeds has not gone up again."

He selected three gold coins from a small pouch that now held only one. Hakim took the coins and started to put them in his side pocket, but his father shook his head.

"Put them in that hidden pouch that your mother sewed inside your trousers," the older man instructed. "There are people on the road who would slit your throat for far less."

Hakim understood what his father meant. Poor Mr. Pawar, their neighbor from the adjacent hut, had been attacked on the road by thugs who had sprung at him like leopards going for their prey. They had jumped right out of the bushes, robbed him, and beat him savagely. Mr. Pawar had been lucky. He was still alive.

Hakim attempted to put that thought out of his mind. He could run fast if necessary. In fact, there wasn't anyone in the village who could outrun him in a race. And he was strong. He felt sure he could carry a heavy sack of corn seeds for a long period of time. The ribs on his thin body were visible, but that was true of all the children in the village. Hakim was sturdy and quite tall. He stood a head taller than all of his friends.

"But be careful, Hakim," his mother said as he prepared to leave the hut. She gave him a small parcel of food and put her two hands on his cheeks. "Be *very* careful."

Hakim nodded and took hold of her two hands. "I will."

Port Dannin was a bustling seaport located on the southeastern coast of Africa. It was only eighteen kilometers from Hakim's village, but those eighteen kilometers were a lifetime away.

A narrow dirt road, if you could call it that, led to the town. When it wasn't choking Hakim's lungs with dust, it was grabbing at his feet with thick, malicious mud. Even so, he was very excited about taking this trip as Port Dannin was full of life, and the shops there held treasures of which Hakim could only dream.

When he reached the outskirts, he stopped for a moment. A feast for the eyes and ears, he thought. Look at all those telephone poles that line the road. In Jontu, there is just one.

Here the streets were alive with people, and carts pulled by both men and horses. There were vendors selling their wares, children hanging onto their mothers' skirts, wonderfully colored garments of red, brown, white, green and orange. Hakim's eyes drank in the dazzling sights. He could feel his heart beating faster. He stood for a moment and watched the women ambling down the street chatting away, interrupting each other; their gay laughter filling the air. Some were carrying infants strapped to their backs. Others had arms laden with burlap sacks filled with various goods.

In Hakim's few visits to the seaport, it had always been alive with people and traffic – both animals and cars – but today it seemed especially active.

Then he spotted the sign in the window of a butcher shop: GOAT MEAT – SPECIAL FOR MARKET DAY. That explained the busyness. Today was Market Day.

He walked along further and stopped at the window of a hardware store. Pressing his nose against the dusty glass, Hakim could see the shiny tools, the barrels of rope, and tall ladders leaning against the walls. At the food market next door, his eyes swept the shelves of canned goods, the bins filled with fruit and vegetables. There was more food in this store than in all of Jontu. A little further down the street was a store that held sewing supplies and fabrics with prints of all colors.

Hakim immediately thought of his mother. "Someday..." he whispered.

He turned and walked down to the main wharf, where he noticed a big freighter at the far end of the dock. A stream of men was making several trips up and down two gangways. The ones headed down were carrying sacks on their shoulders from the ship's hold to the waiting trucks on the dock. A few of the stevedores unloading the ship were no older than he.

Remembering pictures of some of the world's great seaports from his schoolbooks, Hakim thought Port Dannin, busy as it was, didn't look much like any of those other places. In those pictures, gigantic cranes and forklifts were moving the freight on and off the ships. But here, there were no forklifts or cranes, just an endless stream of boys and men, ragged and barefoot, only too glad to earn a few coins loading and unloading cargo.

Finally he turned and walked back into the center of the town. The old tobacconist shop with the torn brown awning seemed to be beckoning. Hakim knew the store well, recalling the rich aroma of tobacco mingled with the smell of sweet candy and gum. He entered the store and gazed at the racks of magazines and newspapers, briefly looking at the pictures on the covers. The headlines shouted out the news of wondrous and important things that were happening in faraway places. He wandered toward the rear of the store, stopped and looked up. He could see the shelves of pads and colored pencils, of writing paper, of all sorts of supplies. Then his eyes grew big as he spotted the shelf that he had been looking for.

On previous trips to Port Dannin, Hakim had come to this store and just stared at the boxes which stood on the upper most ledges – the ones containing computer programs. He studied these boxes, reading and re-reading their names. "I wonder…" he said under his breath.

"Hey," called the shopkeeper who was sitting on a stool behind the counter. Readily visible through his too tight T-shirt was a roll of fat which spilled over the man's belt. His jowls wiggled with every move. He was wearing a torn straw hat, precariously listing at an angle to his head. A huge cigar with a long ash was wedged into a corner of a surprisingly small mouth. Hakim wondered how much longer it would be before gravity took charge and the ash fell to the floor.

He stared at the man.

"You there, boy," the man said with a gravelly voice. "You got money or are you just hanging out? There's no loitering here, boy. Don't you see the sign?" He pointed upwards.

Hakim looked up, then down. The tipped straw hat slipped a little further as the man glared at him. Hakim stood frozen, his eyes glimpsed the fat man's cigar. He wondered which would fall first.

"You want to read one of those magazines, boy? Then buy it." The man rose; the ash from his cigar tumbled to the ground.

Hakim quickly put the magazine he had been leafing through back on the rack and walked quickly to the front exit with his blood surging up into his cheeks. He grimaced at the noise the screen door created as it slammed behind him. Taking a deep breath, he hurried along the main road and took his first right down a narrow side street. Then he slowed his pace as he approached the small shop with two benches on the front porch, one of which was slightly broken.

Hakim could feel his heart starting to pound as he came closer.

He walked up the porch steps, barely noticing the grime streaking the store's windows. He peered inside. What he saw was beautiful to behold.

Through the windowpane were six beige computers, their screens lit in bright colors, words and numbers dancing across the monitors.

Four customers were seated directly in front of the machines, all focusing intently on the screens facing them. Hakim could almost hear the clicking as their fingers flew over the keyboards. Some screens were filled with French words, some with Swahili, but most were in English. Hakim smiled. Mrs. Goma, his teacher, had taught her class in English only, the language of the Internet.

Her husband, Mr. Goma, owned the Internet café. He was a big tall barrel-chested man whose body took up an inordinate amount of space. He reminded Hakim of an enormous bear rearing up on hind legs, though his kind face could light up the gloomiest day with a smile that stretched from ear to ear. Mr. Goma, spotting Hakim, quickly smiled and signaled for him to come inside.

The moment Hakim stepped through the door, a crack of thunder split the still afternoon, and as if some great god had opened a valve, the monsoon rains poured down on Port Dannin.

"Hi, my young friend, you have excellent timing," Mr. Goma said, glancing outside where the rain was hissing on streets.

"Hello Mr. Goma," Hakim responded, his eyes fixed on the wonderful sights in front of him.

"Just want to have a look, would that be okay?"

Mr. Goma nodded.

Hakim quickly surveyed the store, feasting on everything he saw. It was a narrow shop, with just enough room for three computers on either side of the center aisle and a room in the rear that accommodated some supplies; a small kitchenette was against one wall in the back room. He turned and read the sign on Mr. Goma's big desk.

Ten minutes – $1 sixty minutes – $5

Most of the businessmen signed up for an hour. Sometimes, if one of them left with time remaining on his machine, Mr. Goma would wave Hakim over and let him log on.

Hakim took the gold coins out of his hidden pocket and rubbed his fingers over the metal surfaces. Then he wrinkled his brow. Maybe I could, he thought, just for ten minutes. But then he shook his head and remembered why he had walked the long distance to Port Dannin. He returned the coins to their hiding place and sank into the shadows while watching the seated customers typing on their computers.

Outside, the steady downpour continued. The rain fell tirelessly from the heavens and greeted the dirt roads below.

13

Dr. Sanders: "They are mostly curable if we can get to the sick ones in time. Sometimes we're successful, sometimes…"

That's a Goer

HAKIM, WATCHING THE COMPUTERS AND THEIR USERS, observed a boy about his age with very fair skin and wavy blond hair standing next to a seated man. The man had signed off but he still had almost forty-five minutes left on the clock.

"Want to go online?" the man said to the boy.

The boy nodded eagerly. "You bet, Dad."

Hakim couldn't help noticing that the boy's sneakers were absolutely clean. Even the laces seemed to broadcast that they were brand new.

"You'll be okay then?" the father asked as he grabbed the large black umbrella leaning against the desk. "I'm going over to the stationery store to get some supplies and have some documents printed and bound. Then down to the docks to see if the hospital ship's come in yet. Don't want Uncle Peter to find no one there to meet him." The man looked at his wrist watch.

"Ought to be back in about forty five minutes. Are you okay staying here?"

"Jolly good, Dad," said the boy, rolling his eyes.

A moment later, the man left.

Hakim watched as the boy navigated his way around the computer, skillfully moving the mouse across the pad. He was playing a game, concentrating fiercely. Then, sensing Hakim's presence, he looked up.

"G'day mate. Ever play *Unwritten Legends*?"

Hakim shook his head.

"It's a super neat fantasy game," the boy said. "Just smashing!. Takes place in the Middle Ages. You know, King Arthur and the Knights of the Round Table; that kind of stuff. Thousands of kids can play it at the same time on the Internet."

Hakim didn't say anything.

The boy with the strange accent furrowed his brow. "You see, you can be a knight or a wizard or rescue a princess, whatever. I'm a knight right now, looking for the sorcerer's magic sword. What's your favorite game?"

"I don't know," said Hakim. "I've never played any games."

"Really?" The boy sounded genuinely surprised. "Well then, c'mon and sit down. Give it a try. My name's Rudolph, Rudolph Sanders. But call me Roo. Everybody does, everybody except my dad and my uncle that is. Yours?"

"Hakim."

"Have much experience with the Internet?"

Hakim frowned. "Not really."

"Well, stand by, and I'll give you the short course," said Roo. "Interested?"

96

Hakim nodded vigorously, and for the next fifteen minutes, Roo showed him what this new world had to offer. Before long, Hakim was finding his own way.

"I'm so glad you turned up," said Roo. He explained offhandedly that he had been traveling around Europe and Africa for the last few weeks with his father, whose international corn and grain business took him everywhere. Home for Roo was Australia, but he attended school in England. Now he was on vacation.

"If you live in Australia," Hakim said, "why are you going to school in England? Isn't that all the way over on the other side of the world?"

"Yeah, you're right," answered Roo. "But my mother died when I was a tyke, and with my dad traveling all over the world on his business trips, England isn't such a bad fit, is it?"

"Oh, sorry to hear about your mom."

"Well to tell the truth, I was so young then that I don't really remember much."

"What company does your father work for?"

"It's called Southern Continental Corn and Grain Company, SCCG for short. They supply wheat, corn, grains, seeds, you know, all those sort of things."

Hakim remembered the letters "SCCG" stamped on all the burlap bags the men were carrying down the gangplanks of the ships. The sacks had been stuffed full with seeds. "I guess I'm here in town to buy some of your dad's seeds," he said.

"Spot on! When my dad gets back, we'll just go over and take care of that. What does your father do?"

"He's a farmer," said Hakim. "Our family has a little farm about eighteen kilometers from here. It's been very hard for us this year, particularly the corn crop. Many of the local farms were shut down because farmers couldn't keep them going."

He told Roo how some people just packed up and left their farms. But his father thought the problem was the seeds. He normally used some of the kernels from the previous year's crop, but now something was very wrong. There were all these strange beetles around, hard crusty things with shiny yellow and brown shells. This year his father wanted all new seeds.

"Hey, Hakim, there's someone I want you to meet," said Roo, floating his mouse over the screen.

With a few clicks he typed in the password for the Marco Polo Blackberry & Company blog.

"There're a whole bunch of us kids from all over the world on this blog. Of course, you've got to be a friend of one of the kids. My buddy, Marco, who started the blog, doesn't want any weirdoes on, or adults for that matter. It's strictly for kids. There's even a special password. Want to meet them? We talk online."

"I think I'd really like that."

Roo showed Hakim how to access the site. Turning back to the computer, he typed: *Hey, Marco. How's it going, my mate?*

A few seconds later, a message from Marco flashed up on the screen. *Roo, thanks for the help. You gave me just what I needed to know. I was finally able to locate the doctor in Italy for Stephania's friend.*

Marco, I want you to meet my new pal, Hakim.

"Take the computer," said Roo. "Go ahead. Marco's the guy I was telling you about. He's a good bloke."

"Huh?" said Hakim.

Roo smiled. "It means that Marco is a good guy."

In no time, Hakim was chatting away. Marco told him most of the kids met through a school pen-pal project, which they at first dreaded, but later realized was kind of cool.

Roo and I have become great buddies came Marco's message.

Yeah, and what about me?

Someone named Jean-Louis had just logged on.

Marco's name appeared on the screen again. *Oh, meet Jean-Louis from Canada.*

I'll tell you, Hakim, Jean-Louis wrote, *our friend Marco here is a genius at trading in the stock market on the Internet and making lots of money. Read the item I posted about it two days ago. It was so cool, super cool!*

Well, I don't know about such things, Hakim typed out slowly and carefully. *You see, where I live in Africa, we've got some really serious problems to deal with. Our village is hurting badly. People have to go without almost everything, even without food. They actually had to close our school so we could help out on the farms. That's why I'm here in town: to buy some new corn seed. It's been strange this year. The corn we planted turned rotten.*

"My God," Marco thought, "This guy's got *real* problems."

Corn, you said? typed Marco. *Hakim, if it makes you feel any better, Ramon, from Argentina, is having the same problem. He's a pen-pal of my friend, Joey. Hey Joey, where are you?*

A new name – Joey – popped up on the screen. *I'm here, Marco.*

When's Ramon coming online? Haven't heard from him in a while. Could you email him and find out what gives? Doesn't his dad run one of those big agricultural farms? Ask him what his dad thinks about the corn. Maybe we could help, Hakim.

Thanks, Marco, Hakim wrote back. *I really appreciate your concern, but time's short and I have to get going. I'm buying a sack of corn seeds here in Port Dannin and heading home right away. My father needs those seeds and needs my help in the fields.*

Roo got back online. *My Uncle Peter is coming into town on this big hospital ship. He travels all over the world on this huge boat. He also makes major speeches at all these medical conferences. In fact, once he got an important medal: the Order of Australia from the Queen herself for his 'achievement and meritorious service.' That's what the medal said. Someday I'm going to roam the world, giving speeches and saving lives and getting medals, too.*

Hold on now, Marco replied. *I thought you said you wanted to be a lawyer!*

Well maybe a lawyer, wrote Roo. *Or maybe a sports car driver. I wonder, can you get a medal for driving sports cars? I mean if you're really good at it and if you win all the time?*

I don't know about these medals, Marco typed. *We don't have any Queens here in the United States.*

At that moment, Roo glanced away from the computer. "Hey, my dad just came into the store," he said. *Got to go.* He signed off quickly. Looking over the top of the computer, he saw that his father was with his uncle. He rushed over to greet them.

"So," said Uncle Peter, tousling his hair. "Your dad tells me you've become a bloody wizard at computer games."

"Yeah, I'm pretty much of a hot shot, if I do say so myself." He gave a big grin and so did his uncle. "Uncle Peter, there's someone I'd like you to meet. You too, Dad." Walking back to the computer, Roo introduced his father and uncle to the fourteen year old African boy who was standing quietly by the computer.

"This is my friend Hakim."

"Nice to meet you," Hakim said, shaking hands with both men.

Uncle Peter was Roo's father's younger brother. Everyone always said that Roo looked more like his uncle than anyone else in the family and that was just fine with him. Both of them had sandy blond hair, lots of it, and ruddy good looks.

Roo explained to Hakim that Uncle Peter, Dr. Peter Sanders, was part of Doctors Without Borders, an organization that stretched all over the world providing medical care to people in need. If there were a natural disaster somewhere, a health epidemic, or a war, the S. S. *Harmony* would sail off to help.

"It was really fortunate that our ship pulled into port at this time for supplies," said Dr Sanders. "It coincided nicely with your dad's business trip to Port Dannin."

"Isn't it dangerous sometimes?" Roo asked. "I mean the places you go?"

Uncle Peter took a deep breath. He seemed to be looking far away. Then a moment later, he turned to Roo and Hakim and described the time his ship pulled up to a dock where a skirmish had recently broken out. There were wounded people everywhere. He told them that the crew took as many as they could on board, some with gunshot wounds, some with knife wounds. There was so much blood all around. Dr. Sanders was operating around the clock, and all the regular beds became quickly filled.

The nurses and orderlies had to take cots and line them up wherever they could: outside on the decks, in the mess area, even in the storage rooms. Life vests were used for pillows.

At one point, a fight broke out between two of the patients who were from different tribes. They had been lying next to each other on the main deck; before anyone knew it, one of the fellows had his hands clutched around the other's throat, squeezing hard. They were carrying on just as they had before each was injured.

"But we got it all under control," said Dr. Sanders, "eventually. So yes, it's a bit dangerous sometimes, but very rewarding. We also try to treat diseases in these third world countries: diseases like malaria, tuberculosis and dysentery. They are mostly curable if we can get to the sick ones in time. Sometimes we're successful, sometimes…" He got quiet for a few seconds. But then the twinkle in his eyes returned. "So, mate, when trouble strikes, that's when the ol' *S.S. Harmony* ups anchor."

Dr. Peter Sanders loved his work. Roo loved his uncle.

Hakim's eyes grew big as he listened intensely. Then he blurted out, "Are you really a medical doctor?"

"Well, last time I checked," said Dr. Sanders, smiling.

Hakim could feel his cheeks flush, not with embarrassment, but with excitement. "That's what I want to be," he stated. "I wish I could stay in school so that I might learn more but..."

"But *what*, Hakim?" asked Dr. Sanders.

Hakim explained about the poverty in his village, the closing of his school, and the poor harvest this year. It was difficult sometimes just to survive.

The tall blond haired man put his hand on the boy's shoulders.

"I know," he said. "God knows I've seen that before. But why do you want to be a doctor?"

"We have a Sangoma, a medicine woman, in our village," Hakim explained. "She often asks me to help her when she's called on to heal people. She says I have 'the gift.' And when I can help somebody, I... well, it makes me feel good."

Dr. Sanders looked hard at Hakim, then nodded.

For the last two years, Hakim had worked with the medicine woman. She taught him about the differences in herbs. She showed him which ones to use for each illness. She would send him to the woods to gather the plants and help in their preparation.

"Sometimes, though, her medicine doesn't work," Hakim continued. "Some patients would just die. That's why I want to be a modern doctor. I want to treat my people with both kinds of medicine."

Then, as if a dam had burst within Hakim, questions began to pour out. "How do you feel being on a hospital ship and traveling all over the world? How do you become a doctor? What kinds of schools do you have to go to? Do you think someone like me could be a doctor?"

"Whoa there," said Dr. Sanders with a smile on his face. "Slow down a little. Let's start with that last question. It's been my experience that if you want something badly enough, a way seems to appear. Right now, if I were you, I would read all that I could. Everything in print is fair game—thick books, thin books, read anything you can get your hands on while waiting for the opportunity to go back to school. We need doctors. Doctors who think like you do will become the doctors of the future, those who know both western medicine and local folk medicine."

Roo's father, who had been on the computer, suddenly logged off and looked at his watch.

"Listen everyone," he said. "I'm sorry to break this up. I was hoping we could spend more time together, particularly with you, Peter, but I've got problems at some of our processing plants in Emileen. Have to leave right away. Let's go, Rudolph. One of the men will take us to the airport. It's a long drive and the roads are... well, you know how the roads are. Can't chance missing that afternoon flight."

Uncle Peter mentioned that he had to get back as well because the ship was in port for a short stay only.

He turned to Hakim and added, "Perhaps next year you'll be able to return to school."

Roo's father told Hakim that he would instruct one of his agents to take care of the purchase of corn seeds.

"I'd also like to give you a gift of some vegetable seeds from a new interesting pest-resistant variety that our company's been developing. Perhaps you might like to start your own garden, Hakim?"

Hakim smiled and thanked him, then turned to Roo. The boys exchanged information, and Hakim added that he'd like to keep in touch with Marco and all the kids. He'd try to get on a computer next time he came to Port Dannin.

"That's a goer," said Roo.

"Huh?"

Roo smiled. "Oh, I mean, it'll happen for sure."

14

*Hakim: He put down the first infant and
then gently shook the mother, but he already knew...*

S-O-S

HAKIM STARTED HOME, HIS BULGING BAG OF CORN SEED
heavy on his shoulder. The sun was still high in the sky; and with luck, he'd
be back in his village before it slipped beneath the horizon. The thought of
having to make the journey in the dark caused him to increase his pace. He
was glad, however, that the rains were holding back for now, but this *was* the
monsoon season. He glanced at the sky.

Two hours into his journey, Hakim suddenly felt a sharp pain at the bottom of his right foot. He put down his bag. Leaning against a tree, he removed
his sandal and pulled out a long wooden splinter that had wedged into the sole.
Next he checked the sandal. Sure enough, there was a hole in the underside.
Not a very large one, but then it didn't have to be. He repositioned the inner
cardboard to cover the offending gap. It wasn't the first time he'd had to perform such makeshift repairs.

He rose, hefting the sack of corn back onto his shoulder, and peered into the brush, searching for a eucalyptus tree with its thick leathery leaves. The natural oils would be soothing for a sore foot. Seeing none close to the path, he walked further into the brush. He spotted the perfect tree, one with a straight-grained trunk and lower branches that he could easily reach. He put his sack on the ground again and reached up for the branches, grabbing one and pulling it near enough to tear off some of its leaves. The smaller ones he saved to wedge into the edges of his sandals, and the larger ones he placed on the bottom, smoothing them flat so they would cushion his walk.

He was crouching down attending to his sandals, when he heard a faint whimpering noise in the distance. Leaving his possessions on the ground, he walked barefoot deep into the woods, towards the sound.

There, in a little clearing, was an infant less than a year old.

The baby saw him and started to cry while flailing its arms. As Hakim approached, he noticed that the infant's upper body, which was partially bare, was covered in an angry red rash which was slightly raised.

"Oh God, measles," he said softly.

There had been many such cases in his village. Hakim himself had had measles at a very young age. He almost didn't survive. The disease is a killer in poor countries, though once one survives there is no danger of re-infection.

Hakim lifted the crying baby and rearranged the light cloth covering it. "Oh my," he said. "It's a little girl." He cooed to her. "Don't worry, little one. I've got you."

Almost immediately the infant stopped crying. He then thought about his village Sangoma, the traditional African healer. She had told him that it was vital to get water for the sick person. Without water the fever will burn her up. Carrying his tiny burden to where he dropped his belongings, Hakim reached for the water bottle that Roo's father had given for the trip home. He gently dripped some onto the baby's parched lips. The sores were visible as she opened her mouth. Her forehead was burning with the fever.

He walked back to the clearing, scanning the surroundings. A woman was sitting against a tree, her head down as if she were asleep. He jumped back suddenly when he saw her.

Softly he said, "Hello there."

She did not stir. In fact, the only response came from a whimpering second child. Hakim bent close to the woman. The fatal rash covered her body.

Probably the mother, he thought. He called out again to her. She did not move. Putting down the first infant, he gently shook the mother, but he already knew she would not wake up. She was dead.

The second baby looked to be the same age as the first. Twins? He wondered. Has to be. The mother must have been attempting to reach Port Dannin from one of the villages.

Hakim gave the other baby, a little boy, some water. He looked down at the two infants. Both were flush with fever. Then he remembered: The *S. S. Harmony*, yes. If I could get back to town in time...

Both infants were crying now. He had placed them on the ground side by side. What to do? He was already halfway to his own village.

It only took a moment for him to decide that home would have to wait. He hurried back to where he had left his things, looking for certain herbs that were familiar to him, herbs that would bring down the fever. He spotted some Echinacea and grabbed some of the leaves of the peppermint plant that grew nearby. Stuffing them in one of his pockets, he returned to where he had left his sack.

Without hesitation, he spilled the seeds on the ground and put on his sandals. With his empty sack in hand, he raced back to the crying children. The dead woman was wearing a large cloth around her neck which she must have used to carry one of the babies on her back. Hakim took this, along with his own sack, and fashioned a sort of double carrier. Once he gave each of the children a little more water, he ripped some strips of cloth from his own T-shirt, wet them, and placed them on their foreheads. It would have to do for now.

He strapped the infant girl in the pouch that hung over his back; the boy he tucked into the sack on his chest. Casting a quick glance at the trail leading home, Hakim took a deep breath and turned back, back to Port Dannin.

Night had descended by the time Hakim reached the edge of town. The kindly glow from the street lamps and the dim lights in the shop windows looked like stars that have come down for a visit.

He hurried down to the pier. There were no ships tied up along the long dock. He sighed. The lights of the town now seemed more mournful, like dull candles surrounding a funeral bier. Hakim squinted as he looked out to sea. He thought he could still make out a slight glimmer in the distance. *The Harmony*?

For an instant, he had the urge to shout out to the ship.

"What now?" he said aloud. He stood for a moment looking at the sea and then, almost by instinct, started to walk toward the Internet Café.

Mr. Goma was sitting outside on one of the porch benches, the dim bulb hanging overhead.

"Hakim! Hi there, my friend!" he said, wearing a broad smile. "What in the world are you doing back here?"

Hakim stepped onto the porch. As he did, the light bulb started its slow cadence.

"What is this?" Mr. Goma said, helping to lift the bundle off Hakim's chest. "Why, it's a baby!"

"Two babies," said Hakim. He turned to show the precious package asleep in the pouch on his back.

"Asha, come quickly!" Mr. Goma shouted to his wife, who was on the computer in the rear of the store. "And bring some cool water, too."

As she opened the screen door, Asha called out, "Oh my word!" She looked at the children. "These little things are very ill." She lifted the other child from its sack on Hakim's back and turned to her husband. "Come with me. My friend, Lolly, is out back. She can help; we can bathe them."

They carried the children into the café, and Mr. Goma returned shortly with a cold can of soda. "Here Hakim. For you."

As they sat together on the porch, Hakim told how he had found the children in the woods, adding, "I know they're very sick. They don't seem to have much strength, even to cry."

"What are you going to do?"

"I was hoping to reach Dr. Sanders on the hospital ship, but it's already sailed."

Mr. Goma nodded.

Hakim's shoulders slumped as he looked down at the ground. "And I don't know how to contact him."

"What about your friend and his father?"

"They're on their way to Emileen in Australia." Suddenly Hakim looked up. "Mr. Goma, could I get on your computer? There is someone else I'd like to try to contact."

"Of course. Use computer number two over there."

Hakim logged on. The screen lit up, and he typed in the password for the Marco Polo Blackberry & Company blog.

Marco, are you there? He wrote. *It's me, Hakim.*

He waited, praying Marco was online. When he saw the words, *"What's up?"* appear on the screen, he gave a lengthy sigh, not realizing that he had been holding his breath. *It's important—make that very important, that I get in touch with the hospital ship that Roo's uncle is on. You see..."*

He described the last several hours as best he could.

Wow, what a bummer, wrote Marco. *Those kids are really sick?*

Trust me, typed Hakim. *I know measles when I see them. I don't even know if they're going to make it. Their mother's already dead. Look, I can't stay on very long. Mrs. Goma is with the children and she needs all the help she can get.*

Couldn't you possibly phone the hospital ship? added Einstein.

I don't have the phone number, and anyway I doubt they'll put a kid through to an important doctor just like that.

Wait a minute, said Marco. *I've got an idea. I'll ask Roo to get me his uncle's email address, and we could try to contact him that way.*

Hakim could hear the soft whimpering sounds of the babies. He reached into his pocket to get something to wipe his eye when he felt the herbs.

Marco, would you mind emailing Dr. Sanders for me? I have something very urgent to do.

Yeah sure, but what's so urgent?

We'll talk later. I must go.

Check the computer from time to time, wrote Marco, but Hakim had already logged off.

Hakim stared at the black computer screen. Again he put his right hand deep into his pocket. Rolling the herbs around between his fingers, his thoughts went to the village Sangoma.

"Clean them well," the Sangoma had said, "and grind them up very fine, almost to a powder, and slowly pour boiling water over them. Let the mixture seep. Then allow it to cool."

Mrs. Goma appeared from the back of the store with warm milk and some bread she'd soaked to make soft. She walked out onto the porch where Mr. Goma was holding the clean and swaddled babies. Hakim followed.

"There, there," she cooed as she fed the little girl.

After taking a deep breath, Hakim said, "Mrs. Goma, I'd like to use the hotplate or stovetop in your kitchenette, if that's all right."

"Well, I guess," she said hesitantly, spooning the food into the infant's mouth. "But why do you need the stove?"

"To heat up a special mixture of some herbs. It's for the fever."

"But do you know what to do and which ones to mix? From what I've seen, folk medicine really can work, but I myself have no knowledge."

"I was taught well by the Sangoma of our village," Hakim said. "I know what to do. At least, I think I do."

"Okay, but be careful. The coils on the stovetop heat up very quickly."

In the kitchenette, Hakim took out a pot and a clay bowl from the cupboard. Then he walked out the back door, scanning the ground. "Here it is," he said after a few minutes. "Perfect." He went back inside, clasping the rock in his hands. He washed it thoroughly and then put it aside. Next he placed the plants in some fresh cold water, picking out the best of the leaves. After scraping the dirt off of the root that he had found and cleaning it well, he tried to dry all the ingredients.

The water in the small pot seemed to take forever to boil. Hakim put the herbs and root in a clay pot. The cleaned rock made a wonderful grinding instrument, turning the mixture into a pulp. Adding the peppermint leaves, he again mashed the mixture even more finely. At last the water in the pot began to bubble. He slowly poured the steaming liquid over the curative herbs and let the mixture seep for a few minutes. Then he strained the liquid and set it aside to cool.

✶ ✶ ✶

On the other side of the globe, Marco was sitting in front of his computer. He and Einstein were discussing Hakim's dilemma.

If you email this doctor, what makes you think he'll listen to you? Einstein wrote. *What you have to tell him is a bit far-fetched, you know.*

Yeah, I know, Marco responded. *It's not likely that he's going to listen to a kid asking him to turn around a big ol' ship and head back to where it came from.*

You'd have to find a way to make it sound very important.

Wait a minute. You just gave me an idea. IMPORTANT, that's the key. You know when I've read stories of people in trouble on the high seas in the olden days, they'd always send out an SOS signal. I think it means 'Save All Souls.'

That would be SAS. SOS would stand for 'Save Our Souls,' typed Einstein. *Actually, SOS doesn't stand for anything. It's just the international call for distress for all nations, not just English-speaking ones.*

Whatever. I'll start with an SOS in the email. That ought to at least get his attention.

Hey, I remember reading these true war stories. In the old days when then sent important information to a ship, they always used a teletype.

What's a teletype?

I'm not sure, but they used it when sending important messages to big boats back then. I know that.

But I don't have a teletype. Guess I'm going to have to use email, Marco wrote.

Wait a minute. Also, if they wanted to make a message very important, they would write STOP at the end *of each sentence. STOP would, in fact, make the mes*sage sound very urgent.

And so Marco sent his email:

Dr. Sanders, SOS – SOS – SOS!!!

I'm Marco, a friend of your nephew, Roo, I mean Rudolph (STOP).

A while ago you met our friend Hakim at the Internet Café (STOP).

Hakim has just found two sick babies in the woods (STOP). Their mother is dead and the babies might die, too (STOP). They need your help (STOP).

Hakim would like you to go back to Port Dannin right away (STOP).

Could you call the Internet Café and he will tell you all (STOP).

   Your friend,

   Marco Polo Blackberry

15

The Sagoma: "Use the herbs, Hakim. It's nature's way".

The Way of the Sangoma

"WHERE'S MRS. GOMA?" ASKED HAKIM AS HE CAME BACK out to the porch.

Mr. Goma was cradling the sleeping babies. "Inside getting some bedding together. Come sit down."

Hakim studied the sleeping children for a moment and then reached down for one of them. Though still covered in the rash, the baby girl had lost some of the pallor that comes with being desperately sick. Picking up the tiny baby boy in his arms, Hakim couldn't help thinking how pale and listless he seemed.

"How long did you walk with the babies?" asked Mr. Goma.

"I don't really know," said Hakim. "Maybe three hours. I didn't even realize I was tired until you took the babies from me."

Mr. Goma looked at Hakim, then shook his head and said, "My God..."

Just then the phone rang.

"Will you hold her while I get that?" said Mr. Goma.

"Of course."

As Hakim repositioned himself to hold both children, they stirred slightly.

He gazed down. Both had opened their eyes and were looking up at him. He spoke softly to the one child, then the other. "Rest, my little friends. You need your sleep."

First one closed his eyes, and then the other. Hakim wrinkled his brows. His eyes narrowed. The boy doesn't seem as strong as the girl, he thought. He knew that girl babies sometimes were more robust than boys, but he really didn't know why the tiny boy was not responding like his sister.

There's so much I don't know.

The cool baths had seemed to bring the fever of both babies down, but now their faces were flush again.

"You need names, little ones," Hakim said softly. "I'm sure your mother named you, but…well, we'll start anew." He looked down at the girl. "You are now, hmm, you'll be Aba. It means 'born on Thursday.' I don't know what day you were really born, but since Thursday is when I found you, Aba it will be." He shifted his gaze to the boy. "And what should we call you? Let's see…" Suddenly Hakim remembered the picture of the famous naturalist, Charles Darwin, he'd seen in one of his textbooks. "Yes, perhaps if you carry the name of a great scientist, you, too, will learn many things and teach them to your people. So I will name you Darwin."

Darwin's little body just lay there without much movement.

Mr. Goma came out of the store.

"I was just on the phone with Dr. Sanders from the ship. I told him all I knew. The problem is that the *S. S. Harmony*'s been underway for six hours. At best, it'll be even longer than that before they can make port again. Another difficulty is the weather. There's a full gale warning in effect. That means high winds and rough seas, possibly a storm. Turning a ship around in rough seas is a tricky proposition, and with a hospital ship, even more so."

Hakim looked down at the little boy. "Hold on, little Darwin," he whispered.

"Mr. Sanders wants you to get on the computer, Hakim," said Mr. Goma. "He needs some information."

Hakim handed the babies to Mr. Goma and went inside.

✣ ✣ ✣

Can you describe what you saw, Hakim? Dr. Sanders asked once he had logged on. *Be as precise as you can. What does the rash look like; are the babies alert?*

Hakim thought for a few minutes, then began to type his report. *There are sores in the mouths of both babies, in fact all over their bodies. The worse rash seems to be on the little boy, on his lower back. He's the smaller one and seems much weaker. Both children are hot to the touch. I tried to cool them down.*

He continued to describe the sick children and how they had been fed and bathed and how he was making sure they were getting plenty of water. Then Hakim asked, *Is there anything more we should do right now? I'll await your instructions. Excellent,* wrote Dr. Sanders. *It does sound like the measles. Now I would like you to…*

The communication just stopped. Hakim waited a moment. The screen remained silent. *The storm,* he thought. He waited for several more minutes and then signed off. He could hear Mr. Goma's old grandfather clock which was standing against the wall ticking away the seconds. He stared at the blank computer screen,

The fever, damn that fever. The Sangoma came to mind. He could hear her say, *use the herbs, Hakim. It's nature's way.*

He went back into the kitchenette and found the cooled liquid. He brought it to Mrs. Goma. "I think we should give this a try."

The two of them spooned the soothing herbs into the babies' mouths. When the relaxing effect of the peppermint took hold; first the tiny boy closed his eyes, then the girl closed hers. Soon they were both fast asleep. Now that they were settled Hakim asked Mr. Goma if he could check the computer to see if Dr. Sanders was able to leave any messages.

Mr. Goma nodded.

Hakim logged on. No message. Then he went to the Marco Polo Blackberry & Company blog.

Hi Marco, he typed. *You there?*

Hey Hakim, how's it going?

I want to thank you, Marco. I don't know what you wrote but it worked. He then told Marco that he was in touch with Dr. Sanders but was cut off suddenly while on the computer. *And then nothing.*

Nothing? Probably atmospheric interruption, wrote Marco. *They are always saying that on the weather stations. Don't worry. He'll get back to you.*

I hope so.

Good luck.

Just then there was a gentle tap on his shoulder and he turned around.

"Hi there, Hakim, are you finished on the computer?" asked Mrs. Goma.

Hakim looked up and gave a weak smile.

"Why the solemn face?" Without waiting for an answer, she added, "Come with me. It's about time you got something into your tummy, too. I brought some dinner for Mr. Goma out on the porch. There's plenty for you as well."

Her husband was already sitting on the bench eating. The babies were asleep in their make shift little beds made out of dresser draws. Hakim nodded to Mr. Goma and sat down silently. He swallowed a very long drink of water and took the bowl of steaming stew that was set down for him. The aroma of the coriander, turmeric, ginger, and cinnamon spices was irresistible. He had forgotten how hungry he was. He had to force himself not to gobble every-thing down, but the soft yams, zucchini, onions, and beans were the best thing he had ever tasted. There were even some little morsels of chicken tucked underneath. He could almost feel strength returning to his body and his mind.

The spell was broken by Mrs. Goma's voice.

"There's something else worrying you," she said, "something besides the children. What is it, Hakim? I sense that you're troubled."

She listened carefully as he told her about the problems with the bad corn crop. "And now how am I suppose to buy new seeds?" he said. "My father trusted me. He gave me this money, and he doesn't have any money to spare…"

Mrs. Goma took hold of his hand. "We'll think of something, Hakim."

He told her how he named the children. All of a sudden his words came faster and faster, as if a dam had been broken. All the while, Mrs. Goma looked at him with a steady gaze, smiling from time to time.

"Do you think that it was all right, my naming them?" he asked. "Their mother's dead. There might not be any relatives left as she seemed to be making the trip alone."

"I think that's fine, Hakim. As for names, do you know that you have a very special name?"

"I do?"

"Yes, the name, Hakim, means 'wise one' and it also means 'the doctor.' In my opinion, you were very well named, Hakim. "Now, don't you worry. Mr. Goma and I will do everything we can to find some of the children's relatives."

Don't worry. Sound advice, but Hakim knew what measles could do. Three years ago, he had seen small bodies covered with canvas wraps lining the street of his neighboring village.

"I should be going home," Hakim said. "My parents will be so worried. But I don't want to leave the children."

"Hakim, look at me." Her voice was not harsh, but it had that no-nonsense tone of his old school teacher which Hakim knew so well. "Do not worry about those babies; we are here. But you cannot leave for home now. It's dark and I don't have to tell you the road to your village is no place for anyone to be."

"But I have nothing now," Hakim said. "I have no money, no sack of seeds, not anything. The thieves won't bother me."

"You could not be more mistaken," she said. "Those gangsters don't need an excuse to make trouble. They would gladly beat you senseless just for the fun of it, *especially* if you had nothing to line their pockets."

The picture of Mr. Pawar's swollen face came to Hakim's mind. "But my parents..."

"Do not fret," she added gently. "My friend in Jontu owns the grocery store which has a phone. I'll call her and explain everything. I'm sure she'll be glad to go to your family's hut and tell them where you are, and why. She'll also let them know that you're spending the night with us and so, not to be troubled. You can leave for home in the morning."

She put her hand up quickly to stop any protest that Hakim might have. "Hakim, my young friend, listen to me now. Things do not always end up the way we want, but then, sometimes they do work out, just not quite the way we expected. Often it helps to wait till the morning. Most everything looks better in the morning."

Morning came and the sun beamed in on Hakim's face as he rubbed his eyes. He washed and dressed quickly. Then he went to look in on the infants.

The tiny girl's fever had gone down overnight, and she seemed eager to eat something. But the boy's face was still flushed. He appeared to be breathing fitfully.

Hakim helped Mrs. Goma feed and bathe the children. Then he displayed that remarkable appetite for which young boys are famous. Mrs. Goma watched him as he wolfed down whatever she put in front of him.

When he had finished, she said, "My husband's been in touch late last night with Mr. Sanders, Roo's father, and there's an email from Roo waiting for you."

Inside the café, Mr. Goma pointed to one of the machines. When Hakim logged on, he saw that there were actually two emails for him, one from Roo and one from Roo's father.

The message from Roo's father said: "Dr. Sanders, told me you put on quite a show rescuing those little babies; a most remarkable story. Mr. Goma filled me in on the details, and I want you to know that the hospital ship is going full speed back to Port Dannin. Dr. Sanders was sorry that he was unable to answer you, but a storm put his computer out of commission. The ship should arrive in the harbor pretty close to 9:00 A.M. your time. My brother said the information you gave him was very intelligent and quite thorough.

"He added that you're probably right about the measles. His ship's been sailing all over the Sub-Saharan continent, dealing with some ugly outbreaks. What you did was truly heroic, Hakim. I congratulate you. Will you stay in town to bring the children to the hospital ship yourself? I know my brother would like to thank you in person."

I'll be there for sure! Hakim thought. He didn't feel much like a heroic figure, but he certainly wasn't about to leave those children until he knew they were in good hands.

The message from Roo read: "Amazing! Everybody on the Marco Polo & Company blog knows about what you did, Hakim."

Hakim was beaming when Mr. Goma tapped him on the shoulder and said,"Telephone for you. It's Mr. Sanders."

Hakim ran for the phone. He was so excited, the receiver fumbled in his hands. "Hello, Mr. Sanders."

"Well, Hakim! You certainly had quite a day for yourself. I talked at length with Mr. Goma about what happened. He told me about how you threw away your full sack of seeds to use it for more important things. We'll have to do something about that. My company gives wholehearted support to the medical teams that come into these areas when local folks run into trouble. Stopping an outbreak of measles is vital. You played an invaluable part."

"I knew I needed the empty sack," Hakim said. "It was hard to know just what to do, Mr. Sanders, but I couldn't think of anything else. Luckily I still have those new vegetable seeds that you gave me. I kept them deep in my pocket."

"That's fine," said Mr. Sanders, "but I have another idea. The hospital ship should be docking soon. Dr. Sanders will be waiting for you. After you give the babies over to the medical staff, come back to the Internet Café. I'll have one of our people drive you to your village – if the road is passable, that is."

"Oh thank you," said Hakim. "My family must be crazy with worry."

"Hakim," said Mr. Sanders, "I don't know of many people, man *or* boy, who would do what you did. I congratulate you, my young friend. Now would you please put Mr. Goma back on the phone?"

Hakim glanced over at the grandfather clock, thinking about what the best time might be to leave for the waiting ship. He noticed after a few minutes that Mr. Goma was still on the phone. Mr. Goma smiled and looked in his direction.

"You bet, Mr. Sanders," Mr. Goma said. "I'll take care of that. And thank you very much. I know Hakim thanks you, too."

Mr. Goma turned to Hakim. "Well, I'm not sure how interested you are, but Mr. Sanders just authorized me to give you credit for a hundred hours of computer time at the expense of his company."

Hakim looked at Mr. Goma, his mouth wide open. "A hundred hours? Did you say a hundred hours?"

"That's exactly what I said. One hundred hours. Do you think you might find a way to put those hours to good use?" The store keeper smiled as he ruffled the boy's hair. Mr. Goma and Hakim then both started to laugh and he gave Hakim a big hug.

Suddenly a loud wailing sound came from outside the screen door.

" Ahhh…no! Oh please, pleeease…no."

126

16

The little grave was under the shade of the huge Acacia tree.

Tears of Sorrow, Tears of Joy

RACING OUTSIDE TO THE PORCH, MR. GOMA AND HAKIM SAW Mrs. Goma sitting on the bench holding little Darwin's lifeless body. She was rocking back and forth as if to comfort him, but the tears streaming down her face told them everything.

The little grave was under the shade of the huge Acacia tree. Standing side by side were Hakim, Mr. and Mrs. Goma and Lolly. Lolly was holding the robust little Aba who still had sores on her face. After Mr. Goma said some words, Hakim spoke between sobs.

"Little Darwin, your life was too short." He drew in a big breath and let out a deep sigh. "I only wish that I could have done more." His cheeks were moist and he sniffled. He thought for a moment. "Our sangoma has always taught us that the body's spirit lives on. I hope your spirit soars like the martial eagle, sure and strong. Perhaps you are now with your mother." And then almost in a whisper, "She will take care of you. Fly high my little friend. You'll be missed."

Mrs. Goma put her arms around Hakim's shoulders and held him close for a few minutes as he sobbed and sobbed.

At 8:30 A.M. Mrs. Goma and Hakim, carrying Aba, left for the docks. Almost as soon as they arrived, they observed the big hospital ship sliding gently into the berth. When the *S.S. Harmony* was made secure to the cleats on the dock and the gangway was lowered, Hakim saw Dr. Sanders disembark, accompanied by two nurses in starched white uniforms.

"Hakim," called Dr. Sanders. "Let me see my littlest patients."

He took Aba in his arms. "But I thought there were two?" Then, seeing the look on Hakim's face, he knew.

"We tried everything," said Mrs. Goma.

Dr. Sanders nodded. "I'm sure you did." He looked briefly, but intently, with a practiced eye at the little girl. Feeling her head, he said, "Well, she doesn't seem to have much of a fever. She looks like she has a good chance of getting through this. We'll put her on the hospital ship and watch her carefully."

"May I say goodbye?" asked Hakim.

Dr. Sanders handed the baby over to Hakim, who gave her a gentle hug. "Goodbye, my little Aba. Get well and grow strong." He turned to Dr. Sanders. "I didn't know her name so I called her Aba. It's a name for one born on Thursday, the day I found her. Isn't she beautiful?"

"She is indeed," said Dr. Sanders. Then he gave her to one of the waiting nurses.

"I named the little boy Darwin."

"Darwin?"

"I tried to think of a name that would suggest, well, bold and curious, and Charles Darwin just popped into my head. I had read that he was a great scientist who gave so much to the world. I guess it was not meant to be."

"Hakim, you still did a very good job," said Dr. Sanders. "As a doctor, you will learn that sometimes there are things beyond your control. I read your account of the children's condition. That was very well done. Tell me, what did you give them to bring down the fever?"

Hakim told him about the different plants that he used to make the mixture the sangoma had taught him. "The babies' fevers were bad, so I felt I had to try something."

Dr. Sanders nodded. "I've read a bit about some of this folk medicine. You might just have saved little Aba's life. I'll keep you up to date on the baby's progress. And I want you to stay in close touch with me. I know how desperately your family needs your help, but it would be a real shame if you didn't return to school." He paused, looked directly in Hakim's eyes, and added, "Yes, I can see you as a doctor one day. Good doctors are hard to come by, and I have a hunch you could be a damn good one."

Mrs. Goma and Hakim walked back to the café together. Hakim was very silent, as if deep in thought. Mrs. Goma looked over at him, put her arm around the boy, and gave him a gentle squeeze.

When they returned, Mr. Goma was waiting for them outside. "Well, my friend," he said, pointing to the old truck that was parked in front. "Here's your ride. You'll certainly arrive in your village in fine style."

Hakim grinned. Even though the blue paint was barely visible on the rusty old truck, it looked grand to him. He stood awkwardly, looking at the couple. He was about to stick out his hand for a shake when suddenly he threw his arms around his old teacher and then her husband, giving them each the biggest hug ever. Without saying another word, he peeked quickly into the rear of the pickup truck, smiled and with a nod; climbed aboard.

The truck ground its way in low gear past the last rut and finally entered the village of Jontu. The driver honked the horn as they came to a stop. Hakim could see his father racing toward him from the field. His mother and two little brothers also came running from their hut. In fact, it seemed that most of the village was running towards the strange vehicle.

"It's Hakim!" someone shouted.

His mother was holding a cloth to her eye – tears of joy. When Hakim climbed down from the cab, his father took him by the shoulders and gave him a big hug, laughing and crying all at the same time.

"Well, my boy! Look at you. Come. You must be hungry and tired, and yet you must tell us everything."

"In a minute, Father," said Hakim. He walked to the back of the blue pick-up and lifted a bulging sack of corn seed to the ground. Then he wrestled a second sack down…and then a third.

All of a sudden the skies opened up and torrents of water poured down as if someone had just turned on a spigot. But no one seemed to mind. The laughing, hugging, and dancing continued unabated.

17

And Away We Go

Illinois, USA

THURSDAY AFTERNOON WAS NOT AN ORDINARY AFTERNOON. Outside of the school building, the line of sleek charter buses sat poised, and the destination sign in every window read: Chicago. They were patiently waiting to be filled with eager students.

Inside Benjamin Franklin Middle School, the excitement was palpable. Students whispered and passed forbidden notes back and forth under their desks. Even the sternest of teachers found themselves gazing vacantly out the window. For Marco, the tension in the school seemed like that moment before a rocket ship on a launch pad is about to blast off.

A bell rang and everyone headed down to the cafeteria. There was a large, boisterous crowd hanging around the snack bar, which was only open this time of day for very special occasions.

As Marco and Piper walked into the lunchroom, he turned to her and said, "Can you believe it? It's finally *our* turn."

"I'll say," said Piper. "There's definitely something to be said for being in seventh grade. I've watched before as other classes took off for their Chicago trip, wishing like crazy I was the one getting on those buses. What did you sign up for? You know what I signed up for?"

"What?" asked Marco, knowing that he didn't have a choice.

"In the morning, Cindy and I are going to the Chicago Institute of Art, aaaand... you know what the best is? I'm so excited I could die. In the afternoon, we're going on a shopping trip to all those fabulous big stores downtown. Cindy's aunt lives in Chicago; and we've gotten permission to meet her and go off separately, shopping on our own. Is this incredible, or what!" Then, realizing that she was doing all the talking, she asked, "Oh, what did you sign up for?"

"I'm going to the aquarium for the morning tour," said Marco.

"Oh, I'm sure that will be very interesting."

"And then," he continued, "in the afternoon, I'm going to the Chicago Board of Trade, the Commodity Exchange."

"What's that?"

"That's where they trade commodities; you know, they buy and sell things like soybeans, wheat, corn, and oats."

"Hmm," said Piper. "Oats, huh?"

Marco shrugged.

"Sounds thrilling," she said.

✳ ✳ ✳

The sun was just setting as the buses pulled up to the Hotel Fairview near Chicago's Grant Park. There was the usual sorting out as to which students were in which rooms. Joey, Marco, and Einstein, using all their adolescent guile, had persuaded the chaperones to put them together. In reality, there was no need for the authorities to be anxious; after four hours stuffed into a bus seat, just the sight of their beds set them to yawning.

Then there was dinner at the hotel, which seemed interminable, after which, the boys returned to their room, played some video games and settled in for the night.

While he was washing up, Joey said, "Marco, why don't you come with Einstein and me tomorrow afternoon. You know, to the science museum. It's supposed to be really cool."

"Nah," said Marco. "I visited one in Philadelphia. It was interesting, don't get me wrong, but I've never been to the Chicago Board of Trade."

"Whatever works for ya," said Joey crawling into bed. "Boy, tomorrow's gonna to be otta sight. Goodnight."

"Hmm, I wonder how long it is 'til tomorrow," said Marco.

"Well," said Einstein, "it all depends if you're talking about daybreak, and then you have to factor in the time the sun rises, of course, and that changes every day. On the other hand, technically, tomorrow begins after midnight but..."

"Goodnight, Einstein!" called Marco and Joey in unison.

18

All of a sudden the floor became a scene of bedlam.
The yelling and shouting reached a frenzied pitch.

It's Never Boring at the Board

THE CHICAGO BOARD OF TRADE BUILDING LOOMED LARGE in the very heart of the bustling downtown Chicago business district. Marco stared up at it in amazement. After spending the early part of the day at the aquarium, he was glad to finally be here – the place that interested him most.

"See the elevated train tracks next to the building?" said Mr. Barker in a voice that suggested he'd told this story to his seventh grade class many, many times. The Chicago Board of Trade was his baby, and his gray mustache seemed to dance, as it did when he was excited by a subject near and dear to his heart.

"In the old days they would literally bring carloads of grains right up to the door. This is where the buyers and sellers would trade. It was almost like an open auction – wheat, corn, oats, all sorts of grains – bought and sold. Chicago is famous the world over as a center for transporting agricultural and meat products. They would ship and package more hogs, cattle, and pork bellies here, than anywhere else in the country.

The goings-on in the 'Commodity Pits,' or 'Futures Pits' as they are also called, will be quite something to see," he told them. "It is sort of like an action-packed marketplace where traders meet face to face, screaming, shouting, and calling out orders to buy and sell wheat, soybeans, or corn."

As usual, visiting the Board of Trade was not exactly a big draw on the annual Chicago trip, and, in fact, only Marco, the twins, Jim and Jemma, and a new boy had chosen to go on this trip. Marco knew that Jim and Jemma's father worked for an agricultural company, which does a lot of business with the Commodity Exchange.

Probably wants his kids to see what the trenches are like, thought Marco.

As they entered the building, security guards were everywhere. They searched everyone's bags, even the men's briefcases and the women's purses. Each person had to go through a metal detector, single file. For a brief instant, Marco had a vision of those steers he had seen in an encyclopedia being led through a shoot to that place where they become rib-eyes.

"Let's stay together," Mr. Barker said, as he presented the woman sitting behind the desk with a special pass.

The woman pointed to the area where a group of about twenty people were already standing. Walking over to the group, Mr. Barker asked, "Are you folks waiting to go up to the visitors' gallery?"

The man closest just shrugged his shoulders and shook his head. He said something in a foreign language. Then one of the others in the crowd said, "Russian, Russian. No English."

A man who introduced himself as their translator came over.

"My countrymen are here to see how the great American commodity exchanges work, to see for themselves the American system of buying and selling agricultural products."

While waiting, Jemma sidled over to Marco. "So," she said, "is Piper your girlfriend?"

"What?" said Marco. "You're joking, right?"

Jemma was a dark haired girl who was slightly taller than Marco. In fact, she was even a little taller than her twin brother. Now she batted her big brown eyes with extra-long lashes in Marco's direction. "Well," she drawled, "Cindy and I saw the two of you in the lobby of the hotel yesterday afternoon. You looked mighty cozy."

Marco thought back on the brief encounter he'd had with Piper in the lobby. They had talked for a few minutes, and while they both *had* felt cozy, Marco was embarrassed by Jemma's insinuations.

"That's crazy," he said. "She was just telling me about her trip to the Chicago Art Institute. She's definitely *not* my girlfriend."

His face felt flush.

Just then the security guard signaled that it was time to move on, and the Russian translator directed his group to follow him as they walked down the hall to the entrance of the stairwell. In front of the stairs was another electrical security gate. The Russians were waved through first, then Mr. Barker's students. After five flights of stairs, they arrived at the visitors' gallery of the Chicago Board of Trade, or CBOT, as the professionals liked to call it.

Marco's eye grew wide as he looked at the panorama spread out below. In front of him was a very long wall of glass, about twenty feet in length, which looked out over an incredibly large room. He was sure it must be the most enormous room in the entire world, or close to it. It looked like the size of half a football field. There were rows and rows of numbers lit up on electronic wallboards in a variety of colors: red, yellow, and green. Looking below, he could see crowds of people milling around.

The guide from the CBOT explained, "There are actually over twelve hundred people down there. The markets aren't opened yet, but when the opening bell sounds, all those people waiting there, the traders, will go to work. Believe me, it will be something to see. If you look down in the 'pits,' as they are called, you can see that the traders are wearing different colored jackets."

Marco nodded as he saw that some jackets were black, some green, some red, and some people even wore orange jackets with beige colored sleeves.

"Each color," said the guide "identifies traders from a specific company."

The Russian translator was echoing everything that the CBOT guide said in Russian.

"About those lighted wallboards," the man from the CBOT continued. "See those numbers?" He pointed to the ones that indicated the last price of a particular commodity; in this case, it was wheat. "And see that number over there, that was the price just before the last price; the other number indicates the highest price for wheat for that day. And here is the lowest price and so forth. Now look up and to the left to the very large TV screen near the ceiling in the far corner."

On cue, the group lifted their heads to the ceiling.

"It's currently displaying weather patterns over the entire United States," the guide continued. "Soon it will show weather patterns in specific growing regions of our country and then weather patterns in the growing regions of other continents. Remember, this country isn't the only place commodities like wheat, corn, and soybeans are grown and traded. That's done all over the world."

Mr. Barker nodded. "Believe me, kids," he said turning to his students. "Knowing what's going on with the weather is a big deal and I mean *real* big.

If, for example, you're growing, say, soybeans, and it's been dry as all get-out, well, soybeans have a way of shriveling up. And if you just happen to be a soybean trader, you sure do want to know that fact. When there isn't enough of something and lots of people want it; the price goes up. On the other hand, if there's been plenty of rain and a nice mix of sunshine, that's the stuff of a very large crop. And if you have a big supply of something..." He paused, waiting for a response.

"The price goes down," came the collective reply.

"Right you are," said Mr. Barker. "You must have heard of 'supply and demand.' Well, that's how it works. So here everybody keeps a steady eye on the weather."

Jemma moved next to Marco.

"She asked to switch her activity to the Chicago Board of Trade," she said matter-of-factly.

"Who," asked Marco?

"Piper," Jemma answered. "But her teacher said no because all the groups had all been set."

"I didn't know Piper was interested in seeing the Commodity Exchange," said Marco.

"Oh, there's an awful lot that you don't know, Marco," said Jemma, her eyelashes fluttering a few times.

"Huh?"

"Okay," shouted the guide, "here we go."

Sure enough, when the big digital clock flashed 9:30, the raucous clanging of a bell filled the hall. All of a sudden, the floor, which had consisted of a crowd of people just milling around, became a scene of bedlam. The yelling and shouting reached a frenzied pitch. Hands were moving with great speed and fingers were gesticulating their buy-sell dance.

Marco looked down on what seemed like total chaos, but even in all that confusion, he sensed a sort of control, as if all the noise and movement were actually carefully choreographed. *Now that's what I call action*, he thought. A vision of a lavish musical production, with dancers and singers racing about the stage without colliding, came to his mind.

The guide continued. "See those various pits down there? Each one is trading a different commodity. Look at the circular areas with a sort of sunken section in the middle and rising platforms ringing the pit. The people at the outermost rings are on the highest rise so they can see over the heads of the people in the center of the pit."

Most of the action, Marco noticed, seemed to be taking place in the center.

"Now just in that pit alone, the one over there," said the guide, his arm extended, "there are hundreds of people. It's the soybean pit. And over on the right, that's the wheat pit."

"What are they doing with their hands?" asked Marco.

"Another good question, young man. If a trader's hands are open wide facing him, it means he wants to buy. If his palm is extended *away* toward the center of the pit, that means he wants to sell. A tight fist means he wants to go up a penny from the previous price, bent fingers means he's willing to pay a half cent increase, and so forth."

Marco became aware of the traders shouting and screaming and waving their arms frantically to get the attention of another buyer or a seller on the opposite side of the pit. A nod of the head from each trader would conclude the deal.

The lights were flashing on the bulletin boards and changing with each trade. A visitor would be totally bewildered by all the action, but he could not have missed the tension and excitement that filled the hall. The Russian translator seemed to be translating as fast as the guide was explaining.

"Commodities are sold in contracts," the guide continued. "One contract of wheat, for example, controls five thousand bushels of wheat. Now, it cost about six hundred dollars to buy one contract. When wheat goes up one cent, a person who owns one contract is fifty dollars richer. The maximum price that wheat or corn can move is twenty cents up or twenty cents down in one day from last night's closing price. For soybeans, the maximum is thirty cents up or down."

"Suppose someone wants the soybeans so much that he is willing to pay more?" asked Jim.

"They can't," said the guide. "They'd have to wait till the next day. For example, if yesterday's closing price in wheat was $2.50, and today wheat went 'Limit up,' as it's called, the maximum price would be $2.70 for that day."

"What happens then?" asked Marco.

"Nothing happens. All trading stops. Everything comes to a halt; no one can do anything."

"And the next day?"

"Well, the next day they can resume trading, but it can go up only another 20 cents to $2.90, which is 'Limit up.' If there were no sellers, everything would stop again."

✡ ✡ ✡

The Russian tourists seemed to have lost interest in the frantic scene below them and began talking amongst themselves. Their translator shrugged and went over to the side and sat down on a bench. Marco walked over.

"Where in Russia are you from?" he asked the man.

"Oh, this group is from central Russia," answered the translator. "It's the region where they grow the most crops. I myself grew up there."

Marco introduced himself to the translator who replied, "My name is Serge, Serge Brosnik. That name you have, 'Marco Polo,' is quite an important name. He was an adventurer, a discoverer, a world traveler. Is that you?"

"I don't know," said Marco "maybe someday."

Serge told him how he studied English at the university in Moscow and became a translator because "farm life is up before dawn, working the land all day without a break, then home for a small dinner and bed before the sun sets. Too hard. Just work all day – no fun. I don't mind hard work, but when you don't even own the land…"

Marco got an earful as Serge told him that in the old days, the farm that he lived on belonged to the State. His father and the other farmers couldn't plant the things they felt that they could grow and sell. Instead, someone from the Central Planning Commission in Moscow, over a thousand miles away, would make that decision. Most of the big bosses in charge had never even been on a farm. They wouldn't even know a pig from a horse.

"Translating is a much better life," Serge said. "But even though I love to travel and see what's going on in the world, and I like my work as simultaneous translator, I'm anxious to go home after each assignment. Isn't that strange?"

Marco looked puzzled.

"My family," said Serge. "I miss my family."

"Well," said Marco, "I can understand that. But a simultaneous translator, that's neat. Isn't that someone who speaks in one language while translating from another?"

"You got it, Marco. How old are you?"

"Twelve."

"As I thought," said Serge. "My son is close to your age. He's fourteen. He's a very good student. In fact he is number one in his English class. At home I try to speak to him only in English so he'll be bilingual, you know, be able to speak two languages."

"When I go to high school, I'm going to study a foreign language."

"Which one?" asked Serge.

"Probably Spanish. It seems to make the most sense since there're a lot of Spanish speaking people in the United States and, well, if a lot of Spanish speaking people are living around you, it seems like knowing what they're saying would be a good idea. But when I go to college, do you know what I'm going to study?"

Serge shook his head.

"Japanese," declared Marco. "*Ohayo, gozai masu.* See, I already know some Japanese. That means good morning."

"You seem to have made a good start," said Serge with a chuckle. "You show uncommon wisdom for one so young. I wish my son could meet you. I have a hunch you two would get on famously."

"Can he get hold of a computer?" said Marco. "If so, I'd be happy to talk to him."

Marco and the Russian translator were exchanging addresses when suddenly a very loud commotion broke out in the soybean pit. There was shouting and yelling everywhere as arms flailed about. The yelling grew even more intense as the fury of hand signals quickened. The pit reminded Marco of a gaggle of geese, flapping their wings after hearing a shotgun blast. "Buy, buy, buy," they were screaming.

Marco could see the electronic board flashing madly. The numbers changed so fast that soybeans, which had closed at $3.28 the night before, climbed quickly to $3.38, then $3.40, and up and up. In the blink of an eye, the lights flashed $3.41, $3.42, and $3.43. The pit had become pure mayhem. In fact, the action began to take on the aura of a rather violent game, with people pushing and shoving while jockeying for position.

Suddenly, one man in a pale green jacket screamed, "I've been stabbed, I've been stabbed!" He punched another trader in the nose as he clutched his left arm. Actually, with all the pushing and shoving, he had indeed been stabbed in his arm, but only accidentally by another trader who was brandishing a very sharp pencil.

A man with a first aid kit arrived shortly to treat the wound, which was difficult to do as the injured trader went right on trading, screaming, and yelling, waving his arms and trying to buy soybeans. He just wouldn't stop.

The electronic board flashed $3.48, $3.49, $3.50.

Marco remembered what the CBOT guide had said that soybeans could only go up 30 cents in one day, "Limit up," or down 30 cents, "Limit Down." The way things were going on the up side, Marco figured that $3.58 was the highest price it could go. Barely 29 seconds passed and sure enough, the screen flashed $3.58.

Then, most remarkably, there was silence. After all the yelling, the stillness in the pit was unnerving, as if the surf on the shore abruptly and inexplicably ceased its pounding. The floor that had been alive with motion was now eerily still. Everyone was silent; everyone, that is, except for the man with the first aid kit who was finally able to convince the injured trader to let him take a look at the wound. The fellow he had punched in the nose was off to the side with an ice pack. The stabbed trader went over and said something, and the two men shook hands. Everything in the soybean pit was quiet.

"What happened?" Mr. Barker asked the guide who had just gotten off the phone.

The guide turned to the group. "An important government report was just released," he said, "which indicated that there were practically no soybean stocks left in the warehouses, none in reserve. It shook everybody up. They weren't expecting it. This was the weekly 'Crop Production report.' It just came out, and it wasn't good; production was down and now this. So I guess there aren't many soybeans around. With a small supply, well, you can see what happens."

"After today, if someone had owned one contract, how much money would they have made?" asked Marco.

"Well," said the guide, "you have to put up eight hundred dollars to own one contract of soybeans. For every penny it goes up, you earn fifty dollars.

"But soybeans can go up 30 cents, just like they did today," said Jim.

"Yes indeed," said the guide. "Today it went Limit up. One contract of soybeans was worth $1,500 to the owner. Fifty times thirty comes to $1,500. Not a bad day's work, eh?"

Then, as if a choral director had waved his baton, the yelling and shouting began again in the soybean pit. The runners were running, the traders jumping up and down, waving their hands, signaling madly. They were shouting at the top of their lungs. Marco saw the boards flashing again. Soybean prices started to plunge: $3.57, $3.56, $3.55. Down they came: $3.47, $3.46, 3.45.

It turned out that the first report had just been a wild rumor, the kind that can cause panic in the streets—or in a soybean pit. The actual account hadn't even been released. But now an authentic report revealed that there were indeed *plenty* of soybeans. Eventually, everything returned to normal—if anything on the floor of the exchange can ever be called "normal." The pace was still quick but nothing like the frenzy of before. In fact, by the time the visiting hour was over, soybeans were back to trading at their old numbers, hovering around $3.28.

The Russians, clearly delighted with this part of capitalism, laughed and waved their arms in a pantomime of what had been going on down in the pit. "Limit up," one of the Russians cried. Immediately there was a chorus of "Limit up," "Limit up," from his companions.

"This way out, everyone," called the guide.

As they were leaving, he handed each one a booklet entitled "Agricultural Futures for Beginners" and a colored photograph of the entire trading floor. When it was Marco's turn, he asked the guide if he could have a second photograph.

"It's for an interested friend," he said.

19

"Thank heavens you didn't give him the ones with the little roses."
Piper: "No. I felt it would have said too much."

K-I-S-S-I-N-G

BACK AT THE HOTEL, PIPER CAUGHT UP WITH HER FRIENDS,

Cindy, and Caree, who were walking back to their rooms.

"So what happened?" asked Cindy.

"Yeah, tell us," added Caree.

Piper was half-smiling. "I saw Marco in the lobby, looking at this Chicago

Board of Trade brochure. He was sitting on that yellow sofa so I walked over

and just started to talk."

"And…" encouraged Cindy.

"And he told me all about trading soybeans and how they buy and sell

stuff using hand signals. Sounds weird, I know, but then after a while we got

up and started walking toward the elevator and look at this! Look at what

Marco handed me."

"Cool," said Cindy. "Now tell me what I'm looking at."

"It's a photograph of the Commodity Exchange's trading floor. He said it was an extra one. I don't know why he gave it to me."

"Well, *I* know," said Cindy. "He likes you."

"So then I thanked him," continued Piper, "and while we were waiting for the elevator, I told him about our shopping trip and how we went for tea and had little cakes at the royal Palace Hotel. I think I lost him when I started to describe the deep red rugs and the glistening chandeliers, so I switched to talking about the petit-fours that we ate with our tea. At that point we both got into the elevator. He pushed the button for the fourth floor and I pushed five.

"Then he asked, 'What's a petit-four?' And I told him they were delicious tiny little cakes with marvelous icing on top and they taste yummy."

"And?" said Caree.

"That's when I told him I saved one for him, and I gave it to him."

"Which one?"

"I picked out a chocolate one with white dribbled icing and tiny silver stars," said Piper.

"Thank heavens you didn't give him one of the ones with little red roses," said Cindy.

Piper started blushing a little. "No, I felt that might say too much."

"Sooo," said Caree. "What did he say?"

"Nothing. He was too busy eating it. When we reached the fourth floor, he got off, and all I got is this picture."

"Yup, he likes you," said Cindy.

"You think so?"

"Look, he gave you that photograph."

Piper smiled. "Yeah, he did."

Cindy leaned over and whispered a chant in Piper's ear: "Marco and Piper sitting in a tree... K-I-S-S-I-NG..."

Some others girls standing in the hallway overheard them. One said, "Hey, Piper, way to go!"

Piper tried to stifle a little smile.

The girls continued down the hall, laughing and giggling all the way.

20

Anything alive they'd kill. "But what did the children ever do to them? It doesn't make sense," said Marco.

Mud Huts

"T-BONE, FETCH," CALLED MARCO AS HE THREW THE FRISBEE into the air.

The disk glided into a clump of leaves that were piled up on the side of the driveway. T-Bone rooted around until he uncovered his prize. Biting down hard on his toy, he shook his head, his long floppy ears slapping at each other. Firmly affixed to his left ear was a soggy leaf, giving the dog the look of a creature with a rather outlandish growth. Shaking furiously, T-Bone finally rid himself of his ungainly attachment, and leafless, pranced over to Marco.

He stood in front of his master, Frisbee in mouth, tail working like the propeller of a motor boat. His eyes were fixed on Marco's pocket as he surrendered the Frisbee and grabbed his reward. Again the Frisbee sailed into the air, landing near the curb. T-Bone scratched at the toy with his paw, flipping it over to get a better grip on it, and once again pranced over to Marco, clearly pleased with himself and delighted to be playing such a fine game. On the next throw he even performed the ultimate trick: snatching the Frisbee in mid-flight.

All of a sudden the sound of a strange new bark came from the sidewalk. Marco turned. There was a dog of medium size, colored black and white with some copper brown spots. And there at the other end of the leash was Bart McHugh.

"What kind of scraggly mutt you got there?" called Bart, pointing to T-Bone.

"Well, he's part Labrador retriever, got some poodle in him, and I think a lot of wired-hair terrier. His retriever part is really neat. Watch this. Fetch, T-Bone, fetch," Marco shouted as he threw the Frisbee as high and as far as he could. It sailed right across the Blackberrys' yard and onto the wide lawn of the neighboring house. T-Bone darted as fast as he could but watching carefully to see where the landing place would be.

When the time seemed right, he leapt into the air to perform one of his rare midair catches, when out of nowhere, Bart's dog appeared- a black and white blur. Suddenly the dog was airborne. He soared an incredible three feet off the ground, snatching the Frisbee out of the air just above the waiting mouth of T-Bone.

"Way to go, Buckey," shouted Bart.

"Marco, Marco," called Lilly, coming out of the front door. "Mother said there's a phone call for you."

"Yeah, yeah, coming," said Marco. He flipped a biscuit toward Bart's dog.

"He's Australian Shepherd," Bart said. "And his specialty is agility – agility and speed. I've even signed him up for the regional Jumping Competition. Want to try it again?"

"Can't. Got to go now," said Marco, turning towards his front door.

T-Bone, eyes scrunched up, looked from one human face to the other as if he was trying to figure out what had happened. Then, spotting Buckey munching on his prize, T-Bone sat down and unleashed a low, throaty growl, the kind that suggests that all is not right with the world.

Marco picked up the phone. "Hi, Joey, Sup?"

"Get on the blog right away. I've been talking with Hakim; we've got some really big problems."

"How big is a *really big problem*?"

"I'm talking *big* like in *war*," said Joey.

"*War?* Hakim's in a war?"

"Well, not quite, but there's been an attack. Get on the blog. He's been talking to Roo and me." The dark computer screen morphed from black to bright blue. Marco's fingers sprinted over the keyboard, opening the Marco Polo Blackberry & Company web-site. He quickly scanned the previous postings that Hakim had written. Then he read:

> *"There's been a massacre at the village of Wara. When I heard of the killing, I went there to see if I could help. Bodies were lying all over the place. I saw them with my own eyes. They'd all been shot or stabbed to death.*
>
> *"A dead child, just an infant, was lying on the side of the road, the mother's body nearby. Its arm was resting several feet away. I got so sick.*

And now I can't erase that picture from my mind no matter how hard
I try."

Hakim, I'm online, Marco wrote. *How horrible! Just awful. How can this happen?*

Listen, Marco. Sanne, one of the teachers, and I just came to get supplies from Port Dannin. She wants to get on line. It would be better for her to tell you what took place. She was with the children at the time of the attack.

Hello, Marco, I'm Sanne. The other teachers and I were on a trip with the school children. We had walked some distance into the woods and then climbed to the top of a large hill. It was around noon when we heard the noise of rapid-fire rifles or machine guns. I had the children crouch down and hide behind the trees and foliage. I crawled out towards the clearing and peered over the brush. Looking back at our village in the distance, I could see the fires burning in every direction I looked.

Men were circling the huts, swinging long branches wrapped with rags. They lit them on fire and hurled them at the mud huts – all that dried straw. The huts erupted in flames instantly.

Earlier that evening, we came back to the village. There were bodies everywhere. There were animal carcasses everywhere. There was silence everywhere.

What about the government, asked Marco? *Didn't they do anything to help?*

Hi, Marco, it's me, Hakim. I'm back online. As far as the big government officials go, my father thinks that they look the other way. They know what is happening and don't care, or they are too afraid to take a stand.

Marco clenched his fist, banging it down on the desk. "Damn," he said out loud. He then continued typing. *Did they kill everybody? Kids? Women? Old people?*

They spared no one, Hakim typed. *They slaughtered anyone and everything that moved. Anything alive, they'd kill.*

But what did the children ever do to them? It doesn't make sense.

You're right, Marco, it doesn't make sense, answered Hakim. *I've never seen anything like this, but I don't think war ever makes sense. They even put a dead pig dripping with blood in the well. It's undrinkable now.*

Where do you go for water then, asked Marco?

There's a stream about five kilometers away. The older children make the trip twice a day to bring back what water they can. And by older children, I mean eight-and nine-year-olds. Supplies were supposed to get here soon.

One of the officials at Port Dannin told the authorities about the massacre. The United Nations Relief Fund promised to send supplies right away. We had been promised, but nothing happened. And then I saw the news. The thieves hijacked the truck, killed the driver and the man who was with him. Then they took all the supplies—took everything.

I wish we could help you, Marco wrote. *How can we help you? Dead bodies? This is unbelievable. And it was a United Nations truck?*

I don't think the United Nations means a whole lot to these criminals, answered Hakim. *I only hope the UN relief group will send more supplies, and soon. We're desperate for bandages and medicine and a water decontamination system or some of those water purification tablets. The hospitals have a supply but can't give us much. They need it them-*

selves. And now we're into the rainy season, the mosquitoes are everywhere. We need very fine

nets. Mosquitoes carry the deadly malaria, you know.

No, I didn't, thought Marco. Then he asked, *when will you be back online?*

I'll be back in two days. Talk to you then. Gotta go now. The ponies are waiting. Bye.

Marco, typed Roo. *I was following your conversation with Hakim. I know all about*

these towns. My dad's company won't let any of his employees go into many of these areas.

Not safe.

But the people, Marco replied. *They've got to buy food, clothing, and they need water—*

all the basics…

Marco, those poor blokes are flat broke, wrote Roo. *Even if the stuff was available,*

they couldn't buy it. And in the big towns, they're just as desperate. Why, I know for a fact

that even in the big cities, the hospitals are dying for modern equipment. Most of the time

in these small villages, they just barter. You know, trade some potatoes and vegetables to get

someone to put a splint on a broken arm.

When you said the hospitals need modern equipment, what did you mean?

Roo told him about one of his father's employees who had broken his leg
in an accident a while back. When they went to the hospital, they had to wait
six hours to use the one x-ray machine. It broke down twice while they were
actually waiting. Repairing it was an impossible task.

They were just lucky that there was one, even one that was very old and had obviously seen better days.

So while we were waiting for our turn," Roo explained, *this old man came in and— can you believe it— he wanted to trade three chickens for some penicillin?*

Hey, Marco typed. *Suppose you had something really valuable? I mean, much better than three chickens?*

Well then, you could probably get a lot of stuff, if it's something they really wanted to barter.

Yeah, that's it — 'barter!' Thanks. You're always a great help.

I am? said Roo.

Yup! Bye.

21

...trying to see a very important man about a problem,
but apparently you can't see this Mr. Gardner without an appointment,
and you can't get an appointment unless you know him.

The Glass Building

MARCO BIT HIS LOWER LIP. HE LOOKED UP AT THE STARKLY modern glass building with the grey metal doors. He stood there, motionless. It was probably the finest building in the whole town of Lizbet, Illinois.

In an attempt to seem a little more grown up, he had donned his new dressy shoes. He bent down and re-tied his already perfectly tied laces. Okay, he thought while running his hand over his hair to smooth it down. Here I go.

He stood up nice and tall and entered the gleaming glass building.

The marble floors of the lobby had been polished to a high shine. He walked over toward the bank of elevators on the right and looked at the directory nearby. "Hmm," he uttered to no one in particular. "Daniel Gardner, Vice President—fifth floor. Sweet."

He pressed the button and the elevator doors hissed open. Even the floor of the elevator was polished. Upon arriving on the fifth floor, he approached a large table which held a computer, an elaborate desk phone system and a vase with a single red rose. The receptionist seated behind was smartly dressed in a tailored suit.

"Can I help you?" she asked.

She had perfectly coiffed blonde hair and affected a slight British accent. The look she gave Marco suggested he might very well be a security risk.

"I'm here to see Mr. Gardner," answered Marco.

"Do you have an appointment?" she asked.

"No, but I only want just a few minutes of his time, to ask him a question."

"I'm afraid that's impossible," said the receptionist, handing him a business card. "Why don't you write to him?"

"I did, twice, and each time I got a long form letter that told me a lot of things that had nothing to do with what I wanted to ask him. I really wouldn't take any more than five minutes, I promise."

Marco assumed his most sincere look, the one that usually worked with his teachers when he promised to get his late paper in the very next day.

"I'm frightfully sorry," she said. "There is nothing I can do for you without an appointment."

"But I can't get one unless I know him," said Marco, "and I can't get to know him unless I have an appointment."

"I really am sorry," she said. "You must be aware that Mr. Gardner is a very busy man. Actually, I think he's already gone for the day. You'll excuse me now, won't you?" She turned to take a phone call.

Marco sighed. He looked at his watch. It was a quarter to five. He had forty-five minutes before his mother was due to pick him up. Walking back to the elevator, Marco saw the sign for the men's room. He walked over to the door and started to open it when someone on the other side gave a massive push, catching Marco off balance and sending him flying backwards. He landed on the floor with a thud.

He started to rub his sore right hip and backside. The pinky finger on his right hand, which had bent backwards as he tried to break his fall, began to throb.

"Oh wow, so sorry" said the man who had just sent Marco sprawling. "Are you all right, young fellow?"

"Just a little sore," said Marco, wincing as he rubbed his bottom.

Offering his arm, the man said, "I'm so sorry. I have this terrible habit of flinging doors open. Drives my family crazy."

Marco nodded, cradling his sore pinky finger. He tried walking but had a distinctive limp.

"Hold on a minute," said the man. "Why don't you come over here in this waiting area and sit down? That was quite a jolt. Can I get you a soda?"

"Sure, I'd like that," said Marco.

The man returned with the drink and apologized once again for knocking him over.

"Don't worry," said Marco. "Anyway, I think I contributed to the accident 'cause I'm wearing my new shoes. You know, they're the slippery kind."

"Hmm," said the man looking down. "Very sharp indeed. You must be going someplace special."

"Yeah," said Marco. "At least I thought I was. I was trying to see a very important man about a problem, but apparently you can't see this Mr. Gardner without an appointment, and you can't get an appointment unless you know him or something."

Marco held the soda can with only four fingers because his little finger was throbbing.

"That finger is hurting you, isn't it?" the man said.

It was more a statement than a question.

"A little," Marco admitted.

"Here, let me look at it. Hmm," he said, gently turning Marco's hand over. "Could be broken. We ought to X-ray that. You know, we make X-ray machines. We're a medical products company."

"I know," said Marco. "That's why I'm here. But don't worry, my finger's not broken. See, can wiggle it."

"And just why do you want to see this Mr. Gardner?" asked the man.

"I need an X-ray machine," said Marco.

The man lifted his eyebrow.

"Oh, it's not for me. It's for my friend, Hakim."

"And why would your friend, Hakim, need an X-ray machine?"

Marco then went on to explain how survival in Hakim's African village was very tenuous at best, even when there wasn't a drought, and now he was trying to help a neighboring village which was totally destroyed by armed thugs.

"There's actually a war going on there," Marco said, nodding. "The United Nations Relief Fund was sending in supplies, but they never arrived. The driver and his helper were both killed." Marco drew his right index finger across his neck. "Throats slit, I think." He paused and looked into the man's eyes and the man was looking directly back at him.

"Anyway," he continued, "the medicine and food never got there. The kids in this village are really, really desperate. They need food, they need fresh water, they need bandages, and they need anti-malaria pills. I don't know." He shook his head. "They need so much. They don't have anything, and my friend Hakim, he's trying to help. But he's only a kid himself, and he doesn't have any money."

"But why would your friend need an X-ray machine?" asked the man.

"Well, the nearest medical supplies are at the hospital, but the hospital is too poor to spare any. When I heard the hospital doesn't even have an X-ray machine that really works well, I thought I could explain the problem to Mr. Gardner. Since his company makes the machines, maybe he could spare an extra one to send to Africa. Then Hakim could barter, you know, trade, and get the medicine the kids need. Did you know the people there do that all the time?"

"That's a very tall order for such a young man to undertake," said the man. "If you had this machine, how were you going to get it to Africa? Our company doesn't even do business in Africa."

"We just need to get it to Australia. From there I think we can get it to Africa. Does your company do business in Australia?"

"Oh yes, and New Zealand, as well as most of the major cities in Europe. You certainly have been thinking this thing through. That's some story you've got there, young man. What's your name?"

"Marco. Marco Polo Blackberry."

"Well, pleased to meet you, Marco Polo Blackberry," said the man extending his hand. "My name is Mr. Gardner, Mr. Daniel Gardner, Vice President of Operations."

"Nice to meet you, too," Marco said, a slow grin creeping across his face.

22

"…synergy," Einstein wrote. *It's like two plus two equals five.*

Synergy

HEY, ROO, YOU THERE?

G'day to ya, Marco. Told my dad about that village; the one near Hakim's home. Did the gangsters actually burn it to the ground?

Nothing left but cinders.

That's what I thought, bloody miserable crooks. Well, my dad did promise to send some extra bags of grain with the next shipment to the area.

Good job, Roo. But I was wondering, do you think your dad's company could also put an X-ray machine on his cargo plane if we could get one to the airport in Marissallie in Australia?

Maybe, but where in the blazes are you going to get an X-ray machine? They cost a lot of money!

I'm working on that. Your dad's company flies all kinds of cargo into Zakki in Africa, doesn't it?

Yeah, but he doesn't have a whole bunch of X-ray machines lying around.

Okay, I know, Marco typed. *But if we got this equipment to the Marissallie, do you think he could arrange to have it put on the next plane to Africa?*

Dunno, I'll ask. But tell me, what's up?

Well, once it arrives, then it's just a matter of transporting it to the big hospital in the city. Hakim's working on that. He's trying to borrow a truck.

And then... Roo typed.

Remember what you told me about bartering, wrote Marco? *Hakim and I were talking, and I got to thinking about this 'trading stuff.' It turns out that Mr. Goma knows a nurse who is one of the hospital administrators. She has agreed to give us all kinds of stuff—medicines, anti-malaria drugs, bandages, even water purification equipment—if we can get her an X-ray machine. The hospital's desperate for a good one.*

But Marco, said Jean-Louis, joining in. *Even if Hakim could get the truck to carry the supplies, what makes you think the thieves won't rob this one, too?*

Yeah I know, answered Marco. *Major problem.*

What we need is some magic, Jean-Louis who had just come on line. *You know, like your friend Houdini, or maybe we could dream up a fairy godmother who waves a magical wand?*

That worked for Cinderella, Marco wrote. *But she's got to make the truck invisible. We've got to come up with something.*

Actually, if we put all our heads together, we can create 'synergy.' It was Einstein this time. *It's like two plus two equals five.*

Einstein, Marco typed. *What are you talking about?*

It's true. 'Synergy' is when the result comes out better than it would have if each of us worked alone. In a way, it's magical.

Maybe you could hire some armed guards or get some military men to guard the truck, offered Joey, who had also been following the conversation.

How are we going to do that? asked Marco. *It costs money to hire guards, and as far as any military help, Hakim told me that sometimes these criminals steal the uniforms and dress up like soldiers. In fact, Hakim's not sure if some of the soldiers themselves aren't stealing the stuff.*

Camouflage, announced Einstein. *That'll do it.*

Hello, Marco, it's me, wrote WanTing, who had just signed on. Auntie M. had introduced the two of them online as she had met WanTing on her travels to China.

I've just read all about Hakim's problems on the previous postings. I'd like to help.

Well, Marco answered. *Do you have some camouflage paint? Ha, ha!*

No, WanTing replied. *But I can help provide some netting.*

Netting?

Yes, for the mosquitoes. You know, to avoid malaria. We do very fine weaving at our factory in Haon. It's not very modern, but you'd be amazed by the excellent work we can produce. I'll ask if the owners might let my friends and me make some special nets. If the children sleep under these mosquito nets, they can have protection. Hakim did say they were coming into the rainy season.

That's true, Einstein wrote. *Malaria's a real killer all over southern Africa. I read that one million people get infected each year and a third of them actually die, mostly children.*

And the netting, asked Marco?

You put the netting around the beds so the children don't get bitten at night when they're sleeping, Wan Ting explained. *Though the nets aren't foolproof, at least it will give them some protection.*

Now we're on a roll, Marco wrote. *All right, let's see: we have some netting, we have some bags of grain, and maybe we can trade an X-ray machine for medical supplies. Not bad.*

Yeah, but we still haven't figured out a way of getting the stuff to the village without getting it ripped off, added Einstein. *I maintain unequivocally the only solution is camouflage!*

Clearly, we've got more thinking to do, Marco told them. *How 'bout everybody posting their ideas here on the blog. I'll try to find out when Hakim can get online so we can coordinate everything. But don't be afraid to go wild with your thoughts. Use your imagination. 'Think outside the box,' as they say! Think way outside the box.*

"Piper, don't you ever get online?" Marco said into the telephone.

"I'm so busy right now," Piper said. "I'm in the middle of a big art project for school. The cuttings are all over the floor. I have red ink on my cheek, and up to a minute ago, my right index finger was pasted to the left sleeve of my shirt. It's a collage, and it's got to be finished by Friday. So what are you up to? Please tell me that you occasionally have homework, too."

"I do, I do, but right now we've got bigger problems. Hakim's trying to help a village that's been destroyed, just wiped out, and lots of people killed—even kids. Honestly, those thugs are a bunch of animals. They burned down all the houses, too."

"You mean *blew* down," said Piper. "I distinctly remember the wolf *blows* their houses down."

"Piper!" Marco shouted, his anger surprising him. "We're not dealing with a fairy tale here. There were *people* in those huts, some of them just babies, and they were all burnt alive, Piper, *alive!* So no more with the fairy tales, okay?"

"My gosh, Marco, you mean, this is for *real?*"

"Yeah, as real as it gets. Some people managed to escape into the woods. Then the survivors started trickling back to Wara. Everyone is desperate for food. Hakim went there to try to help. He even organized the older children to form a little water brigade."

"Marco, I'm so sorry. I guess I'm a little too sarcastic for my own good. Is there something I can do to help?"

"I had a thought," said Marco. "Can you and your friends get some stencils from art class and draw some very large letters and symbols that we could cut out and paint? I need some type of sign."

He continued telling her his idea.

"I got it," said Piper. "I know exactly what you want. Only I think there's a better way to do it. Just leave it to Cindy, Caree, and me. But tell me, how are you going to get all of this stuff to Africa?"

"I don't know," Marco said, scratching his head. "Carrier pigeon?"

23

Camouflage

Africa

THE RUNWAY LIGHTS CAME INTO VIEW. THE PILOT SET THE plane down with a gentle screech. It was dusk and the red glow of twilight was still visible on the western horizon. As the engines of the plane were turned off, the sounds of the African night took over—insects and frogs and occasionally, a mournful wail from God knows what and from God knows where.

Cargo handlers in tan-colored jumpsuits swarmed over the plane, unloading supplies from the regular shipment of Southern Continental Corn and Grain. They heaved the boxes and crates onto waiting official transport vehicles.

Almost imperceptibly from the side of the runway, an old rusty grey truck appeared; some parts of it seemed to be dangling from below. It rumbled up to the plane at a very slow pace like a grumpy old man bent over with a cane, carefully picking his way in the dark ever so quietly. One could barely make out the faded red hospital insignia on its sides.

A half hour later, several additional bags of grain, a large bundle with Chinese writing on the top, and two X-ray machines were unloaded from the cargo bay of the plane onto the waiting truck. There was also one flat box with strange lettering on it: "Tohpt vu ci qmedif up vsadl."

Hakim knew right away what the apparent gibberish meant. "Signs to be placed on truck." He had been expecting this package. He knew the language would be nonsensical to any casual reader, but for those who knew the code, the sign was crystal clear.

Nebo, an eighteen-year-old, was tall—well over six feet—and very skinny. He was from Hakim's village and had agreed to help in spite of the danger involved. He was needed for many reasons, not the least of which was that he knew how to drive.

"What were those funny letters written on the box?" Nebo asked.

"It's a code," Hakim said, allowing himself a smile. "My friends and I came up with it."

"How do you know what it says?"

"Simple. When you want to put a word into code, just use the next letter in the alphabet, with the exception of vowels. If you want to use a vowel, then you choose the next vowel in alphabetical order."

"Huh?"

"For example," said Hakim, the word C-O-D-E- would be written with a D (for the letter C), U (for the O), F (for the D, skipping over vowels), and I (for the E).

'Code' becomes 'Dufi.'"

"Great," Nebo said. "So my name would be … P-I-C-U?"

"You got it! And mine is Jelon. We can have fun with the code later, but for now we've got to concentrate on what we are doing.

"You're right," said Nebo. "Concentrate."

Nebo sat erect and alert in the driver's seat of the battered old truck. Hakim sat next to him on the passenger's side. Nebo could feel the palms of his hands grow moist as he drove from the airport to the city hospital. Without turning his head, his eyes darted left, then right. The two did not talk as they drove the three miles into the center of town, constantly scanning the darkness.

Hakim pulled the old straw hat he had brought with him down further on his head, all the while peering out from underneath. He had hoped that by wearing such a hat, he would look more grown-up than his 14 years.

When the signs for the hospital entrance appeared, Nebo steered the vehicle carefully around to the delivery entry at the back of the building. Clouds had slowly glided across the night sky, obscuring the moon. The night had turned pitch black, a phenomenon for which both Hakim and Nebo were grateful. Nebo had already turned off the headlights, and despite the sounds that very old trucks emit, the vehicle continued on its way slowly but without provoking undo attention.

They parked at the farthest side of the loading dock as they had been instructed. Only one small bulb illuminated the dock. Hakim suddenly realized he'd been holding his breath. He unclenched his fists as he slowly exhaled and looked over at Nebo, smiling gently. "Are you okay?" asked Nebo.

"Yeah, I'm fine," Hakim said. "Just thinking I'm awfully glad you're here."

Nebo returned the smile. Then, stopping the truck he jumped down and gave his pants a yank up as the flimsy belt threatened to drop.

"Got the note?" he asked.

Hakim nodded, taking the folded paper out of his pocket and handing it to the older boy.

"You wait for me here," Nebo said.

Hakim watched as his lanky friend climbed the four cement steps leading to a narrow wooden door. Nebo knocked. After a moment, a long, long moment, someone inside unlatched the door. It swung open and Nebo disappeared inside. Hakim pulled his jacket tightly around his chest and turned the collar up against the chill of the African night. He began counting the faint clicks of the cooling truck engine. By pure effort, he thought of a time when, long ago, he had been swimming in the stream that ran by his village. The day had been blistering hot and the water was deliciously cool. He was then jolted out of this peaceful reverie by the sound of a rat scurrying across the landing dock. He was back to the still, deathly quiet night.

Ten minutes later, or was it ten hours, Nebo returned.

"Okay," Nebo said. "Here's the reply they wrote out. Is everything right?"

Hakim read the note:

Aqup sidioqv uq vxu y-sez nedjopit, xi xomm

fimos vji gummuxoh:

Upi deti ug tzophit

Upi desvup ug cepfehit op ettusvif

tobit

E xevis gomvsevoup tztvin

Vxu fubip qedlehit ug xevis qasogodevoup

vecmivt

Guas cuyit ug 'qmanqz pav' (150 qedlivt

op e cuy)

Vjsii cuyit ug epvo-nemesoe vecmivt

Esi xua siefz vu neli vji iydjephi?

He wrote the translation just above each of the encryptions:

Upon receipt of two x-ray machines, we will deliver the following:

Aqup sidioqv uq vxu y-sez nedjopit, xi xomm fimos vji gummuxoh:

- One case of syringes
  Upi deti ug tzophit
- One carton of bandages in assorted sizes
  Upi desvup ug cepfehit op ettusvif tobit
- A water filtration system
  E xevis gomvsevoup tztvin
- Two dozen packages of water purification tablets
  Vxu fubip qedlehet ug xevis qasogodevoup vecmivt
- Four boxes of 'plumpy nut' (150 packets in a box)
  Guas cuyit ug 'qmanqz pav' (150 qedlivt op e cuy)
- Three boxes of anti-malaria tablets
  Vjsii cuyit ug epvo-nemesoe vecmivt

Are you ready to make the exchange?
Esi xua siefz vu neli vji iydjephi?

Hakim then wrote a quick message back, saying simply, "Siefz vu hu!"

Two hospital workers helped to unload the X-ray machines and then repack the truck with the promised anti-malaria medicines, syringes, bandages, a whole range of things, even "plumpy nut," a nutritional supplement used for starving children. Most important, though, was the water treatment equipment.

With the truck fully loaded and the workers gone, Hakim turned to Nebo.

"Now for the camouflage."

The two teenagers pulled the flat box from inside the truck. With only the illumination of the singular light bulb dangling above the hospital cargo bay, they removed the contents, laying it on the ground. It had been folded several times so when it was fully extended, it ran the length of the entire vehicle.

Peeling each letter carefully from its backing, Hakim and Nebo put the self-sticking black laminated letters onto the truck. They duplicated the procedure for the other side. Then they unfolded the larger package which contained a very big piece of "strip and stick laminate" in bright red. Hakim opened it and found that it was already cut into shapes. All they had to do was peel off the individual shapes from their backing and stick it on to the truck as the diagram indicated. Now they were ready to go.

The night remained extremely dark as the ancient vehicle wheezed and clanked its way out of the city, rumbling onto the dirt road leading to Wara. It would be a full ten hour drive.

Only an hour and a half into the trip however, a van pulled up alongside. It was hard to see much through the dirty windows, but the men in the van appeared to be gesticulating wildly and arguing with each other. Though the dusty road was barely wide enough for two vehicles to pass, the van continued to travel alongside them for some time.

"Just look straight ahead," said Nebo. "Do *not* make eye contact with them."

Suddenly the van pulled ahead. Hakim tried not to stare, but he couldn't help noticing several sets of eyes glaring out of the back of the vehicle.

Two hours later, they came upon a burning truck on the side of the road. Whoever had been driving it was nowhere in sight.

"Do you think those guys in the van had anything to do with this?" Hakim asked.

"You can bet on it," said Nebo.

Hakim thought he could make out some lettering on the side of the truck as they slowly passed:

HENZACH Machin – equi –

The letters were barely readable, and now with the smoke, it was hard to see, but it was enough. They didn't speak for some time.

Seven long, dusty, jolting hours later, they arrived at Wara, or all that was left of it. Hakim and Nebo climbed down from the truck, stretched as long and hard as they could and walked stiffly around the vehicle before starting to unload the packages.

Then, appearing from nowhere, came six adults and twenty children at least, who slowly gathered around, scratching their heads and shrugging their shoulders at this strange apparition that had come rumbling into their village.

The writing on the sides of the truck in black letters stated: **Danger, Contamination, Biohazard.** In large red laminate was the international symbol for dangerous biological materials and one for radiation.

Slowly, carefully, the boys unloaded the water filtration equipment, and then the precious medical supplies: anti-malaria pills, antibiotics, bandages, antiseptic wipes. There were also hospital sheets and blankets, several large bags of corn seed with SCCG printed on the side, and a very strange package with some funny lettering that no one could read.

"Ah," said Hakim, noting the Chinese characters written on the side. "Here it is. Way to go, WanTing!"

He unwrapped the package with trembling hands. And there lying on the ground, was very fine mosquito netting to surround the beds of the children; netting to fend off the malaria carrying mosquitoes.

Spontaneously, the crowd that had gathered began to clap softly and in unison.

24

"My brother's been sick with running stomach for ten days." Letter from a child.

Letters from Afar

Illinois, USA

I BIT SO HARD ON THE INSIDE OF MY CHEEK THAT I COULD taste blood.

So began Hakim's posting. He told everyone about the van with the men inside, holding guns. He said he kept picturing two graves, his and Nebo's, but Nebo just kept driving and telling Hakim to look straight ahead. Luckily, the windows were so dirty that when Hakim ignored Nebo's advice and took a peek, the men didn't see him. Perhaps it was because the hijackers were too busy arguing among themselves, flailing their arms around and shouting to each other.

I'm telling you, Marco, Hakim wrote. *I was shaking the whole time the van was alongside of us. Then, all of a sudden, it raced ahead, spewing a great cloud of dust. I don't know if any of those gangsters could read, but one of them apparently did know what the biohazard symbol meant. That was incredible! Without your plan...*

Well, I must admit, answered Marco, *everyone gave their ideas, but the camouflage, yes, I did like that one. You guys, though, were way cool. I guess villagers got all that good stuff, right? They got it all right; but Marco, these people need more.*

Hakim described the constant need for more food, more blankets, more clothing, and more medicine. *The people need chickens and livestock,* he wrote. *They need more of everything! Some people from Port Dannin are trying to help to rebuild the huts, but there's too much to do. The people are desperate.*

While reading and re-reading Hakim's postings, Marco smiled. *Hold on there, buddy,* he mused. *I hear you. I'm going to see what I can do. There's a friend of mine I'm going to visit tomorrow.*

"That's some incredible story," said Daniel Gardner the next day while pacing in front of his desk. "And I'm sure you're right about what those poor folks need. If it were just up to me, the villagers would get every damn thing on that list.

But Marco, I don't own this company, and there's only so far I can go. My department has money for things like this, but it's finite, and I'm afraid we've used up all of our allotment. You'll have to find some other way; you'll have to find some way to raise money. It breaks my heart Marco, but…"

"Well, thank you anyway for all the help you did give, Mr. Gardner," said Marco. He didn't realize it, but he was biting his lower lip.

"Good luck to you young man," said Mr. Gardner.

Marco pushed the grey doors of the big glass building open and headed down the front steps. The words "some way to raise money" kept resonating in his mind.

Once home, Marco got on his computer. Within minutes, he was online with his buddy, Roo.

So what did your father say, Roo?

It's a bummer. He said they were glad to help once, but this couldn't be a regular event. The company is not in the charity business, you know. He said he's supposed to make money. Hey, maybe we could get other companies to donate stuff?

Yeah, Marco wrote back. *But then we'd have to pay to charter a plane, and now we're talking big bucks.*

Marco, it's me, Piper. Sorry to break up your conversation but did you see those letters we got from the children in Wara? Hakim emailed them to us.

What letters, asked Marco?

Piper forwarded the letters to him, and Marco leaned close to the screen and started reading.

Dear Kids from Marco Polo Blackberry & Company,

I am eight years old. My teacher is helping me write this letter. Our friend Hakim has told us all that you have done to bring food and medicine to our village. Thank you. Last week my parents and grandparents were killed. So was my baby sister. They didn't do anything to hurt these soldiers. I don't understand.

Bye, Fola

Dear Friend,

The gunmen came to our village and took everything we had. What they couldn't take, they burned. My six-year-old brother and I are all that is left of our family. We were lucky as we were on a trip with the school. My brother has been sick with "running stomach" for ten days. He has been coughing. I hope this medicine you sent us will help.
Thank you.

Hello,

Both my parents were killed in this raid on our village. My two sisters and I only have the clothes that we were wearing that day. We have nothing, no family. We feel so sad. Then the truck came with all those wonderful things. Thank you and Hakim and all your friends for helping us. Tonight for the first time, my sisters and I will sleep under the mosquito nets. Several children died last year of malaria in our village. The rains are already here. It is good to have the netting.

Your friend,
Mallaki

Do they grab you or what? wrote Piper.

Marco didn't respond for almost a full minute.

Marco, Marco, typed Piper. *Are you still there?*

Yeah, I'm here. I'm just thinking, really thinking.

PART III

25

*Uncle Horace: "Truth is, we've been having quite a time with our corn crop.
Some insects are munching away at it."*

Uncle Horace

"HEY THERE, T-BONE, YOU 'OL MUTT," SAID UNCLE HORACE.
"Am I on time for dinner?" The dog cocked his head like he was trying desperately to figure out how this guy knew his name. "Don't look at me that way, dog,"
said Uncle Horace. "Your mama is *my* dog. You were born on *my* farm."

"He's a great dog, Uncle Horace," said Marco.

"Truly one of the great canines of the Western World," added Mark
Blackberry, Marco's father. "He's become a bona fide member of the family. I
feel as if I have three children now. But this one not only obeys me; he brings
me the newspaper."

"And he likes to go for rides with me, don't you, T-Bone?" said 5 year old Lilly.

Marco felt the same frustration that always overwhelmed him during his
Go Fish games with his little sister. No matter how many times he tried to
explain that a Jack and a Queen do not make a pair, she would insist, "Yes, they
do. They're both pictures." Marco could only shake his head.

"My doggy and I go riding together all the time," Lilly affirmed once again.

"He isn't your dog," said Marco, glaring. "And he doesn't go riding with you."

"Yes, he does, he does!"

"Marco," said Uncle Horace, "she's just a little girl with a vivid imagination. I think it'd be a really good idea to let it go for now, okay?"

✳ ✳ ✳

At dinner Auntie M. commented, "So nice to see you again, Horace. But where's Helen?"

"Oh, she doesn't much care to join me on my business trips," said Horace. "The only reason *I'm* here is that I'm heading up a committee in Champlain."

"And what committee might that be?"

"It's the *'International Scientific Conference on Pests in Agriculture.'* Starts tomorrow bright and early."

"That's a mouthful," said Auntie M. "Just what is this conference about?"

"We wage war on pests, all kinds of pests: big ones, little ones, beetles 'n bugs and bad, bad children."

Lilly giggled. Marco smiled.

"Well, how's everything going on the farm?" asked Mark Blackberry, putting some rare roast beef on his fork.

"Not looking as good as T-Bone, I can tell you that. The truth is we've been having a heck of a time with our corn crop. Some insects are munching away at it. The husks look healthy enough, but when you peel 'em back, you're lucky if you can find five intact kernels on the entire cob. I even called in my friend, Dr. Brody. He's an entomologist from Iowa State.

"When the problem first started, Tom—that's Dr. Brody—took some samples back to his laboratory to analyze. He said he hadn't seen anything like this before. He has been working on the problem ever since with some doctor from overseas. So, now things aren't looking too rosy for this growing season."

"Hey, that's weird," said Marco. "I heard about a problem with corn from my friend, Roo, in Australia, and also from another friend in Africa."

"Marco," said his father, raising his eyebrows.

"Well, that's what my friends told me, Dad."

"That's nice, Marco," said his mother, "but your father and Uncle Horace are talking. You know what I've told you about interrupting adults when they're talking."

"How come *he* knows about this corn stuff?" asked Lilly. "If Marco knows, why can't I?"

"Lilly," said Mother, "why don't you come with me into the kitchen and help me put some whipped cream on the strawberry shortcake."

"Okay," said Lilly, jumping up from her seat, clearly more interested in strawberry shortcake than agrarian issues.

"I'll give you a hand as well, Margaret," said Auntie M.

Marco remained, listening intently as Uncle Horace explained the pest problem to his father.

"Actually Mark, Marco is onto something. There might be problems all over, as these insects seem to be affecting corn crops in countless places around the world. In any event, many scientists are descending on Champlain next week for the conference, and I'm stuck with coordinating the speaker program."

Marco shot his uncle a look of unmitigated gratitude and then said, "Dad, would you excuse me from the table? I've got a ton of homework."

Just then, Mother walked in, carrying the strawberry shortcake, followed by Auntie M. and Lilly. "Marco," she said, seeing him leave. "Are you feeling all right? I've never seen you turn down strawberry shortcake for homework before."

"I know, Mom, but I really do have loads of stuff to do: twenty wicked math problems, a history paper to write, and…."

"Can I have his piece?" asked Lilly.

26

*At that moment, Marco looked a lot like the cat who realized that
no one was guarding the canary cage, and that the cage was w-i-d-e open.*

C-O-R-N

SECURE IN HIS ROOM MARCO PLUNKED HIMSELF DOWN IN HIS
desk chair, turned on some music, booted up his computer, and logged on. He
was glad to find Jean-Louis online.

Wassup? Jean-Louis asked.

I'm thinking of trading again-on the Internet, Marco typed.

*Huh? Are you nuts? The gold prices have all gone flat, nothing's doing. Pago-Global is
just dead in the water.*

I'm not thinking of Pago-Global, replied Marco. *Actually I'm not thinking of stocks
at all. It's commodity trading I have in mind.*

What's commodity trading and what do you know about it, asked Jean-Louis?

*I know some stuff. I was at the Chicago Board of Trade on a school trip. That's where
they trade soybean and corn futures. I saw them do it. Anyway, I said I was just thinking
about it. I haven't decided to do anything.*

What's that you're thinking about, asked Joey, who had just logged on?

Nothing, just thinking, wrote Marco. *Hey Joey, did you contact your pen-pal, Ramon, yet?*

You mean 'Ramon the Bandito,' asked Joey? *Yeah, he told me all about the problem, and just like you said, I told him to get on the blog. He ought to be here any...*

Hola, mi amigos, typed Ramon. *I saw that last comment, Joey. Bandito indeed! I just rounded up some of the calves that had wandered over to the next farm as I told you. I put them back into our pen where they belonged.*

Yeah, right, typed Joey. *Bandito, bandito.*

Just you wait Joey, mi amigo, replied Ramon. *One day I'm going to have a ranch of my own with about 300,000 head of cattle, and when that day comes, mi amigo, this bandito is going to invite you down to Argentina so you can count 'em.*

Marco broke in on the conversation. *Hey, guys, I need to get some important info. Ramon, Joey forwarded me your email. Are you sure about what you heard? You're dead sure?*

Absolutely, answered Joey. *Ramon said he's positive.*

Okay, but I'd like to hear it directly from the horse's mouth. Ramon?

Well, I don't know about your "talking caballos;" but I have heard a lot of people saying things like el grano, the corn, is espantoso, terrible. They think that some kind of bug has been eating the kernels.

Is anyone doing anything about it, asked Marco?

Well, all the farmers in our area are having a meeting tomorrow, Monday morning. My father and a couple of the other owners organized it. Some government officials will be talking with them. It might even be on television. And, mi amigos, I'm going to stand right near my father when he's being interviewed. He's the head of our Regional Corn Growers Association.

I don't know if you'll get this on the TV news in the United States, but if you do, look for me. I'll give the Marco Polo Blackberry & Company signal, if I can remember.

Way to go! Joey wrote. *Flash all the fingers of both hands.*

Yeah Ramon, added Marco. *Just open both fists and flash them wide—all ten fingers, which is our signal. Now, I've got something to do, guys. Got to go.*

Marco logged off the blog. He then went into the search engine of his computer and typed:

C-O-R-N

First, he read about the National Corn Farmer's Alliance. Next he learned how corn grows, and then some uninteresting stuff from the Organization of Corn Refiners. He even noticed there was some news about a "Mr. Eric Corn."

There were reports from a few days ago entitled: "How Slowing Demand and Higher Acreage Might Affect this Year's Corn Crop" and "Sluggish Demand Causes Drag on Current Corn Price."

Nothing in the news, Marco thought. Nothing at all. Not one remarkable thing about corn was reported anywhere.

Suddenly his eyes grew wide. *I wonder what's going to happen when everyone finds out about those corn-eating bugs,* he thought.

His mind wandered back to that day at The Chicago Board of Trade, when the guys in the soybean trading pit thought there weren't any soybeans. *The place went berserk,* he remembered, *and the prices soared. Wow, that was exciting!*

"Well, now how about *no* corn and *no* crop?" he said aloud. "Wonder how that's gonna sit with the 'boys in the pit?'"

He pictured the chaos and confusion that *that* news would spawn. Then, he narrowed his gaze and the corners of his mouth started to turn up slightly. If anyone had seen him at that moment, they'd be sure he looked a lot like the cat who just noticed that no one was guarding the canary cage, *and* the cage was w-i-d-e open.

Rubbing his hands together, he imagined himself at the start of a race. "Get ready, get set…" But then he told himself, "Don't rush it. Tiny steps, tiny steps."

Next, he left a message conspicuously labeled URGENT for Roo.

✧ ✧ ✧

Sure enough, the next morning Roo was on the blog.

Are you there, typed Marco?

Evening, mate, Roo replied. *Or should I say g'day to you, Marco. Forgot about those pesky time zones. Must be mighty early for you.*

Yeah, Marco wrote. *Listen, there's something I have to do before I go to school. Could you tell me all you know about the corn situation that you mentioned earlier?*

Sure, though I don't know a whole lot of the details. The growers seem to be bloody well having a hell of a time from what I hear.

Has anything come out in your newspapers yet?

Dunno, Roo typed. *But there's a lot of talk going around.*

And what are they saying?

Can only guess, mate. Nothing's been on the telly yet.

Telly, asked Marco?

Yeah, the TV, Roo explained. *I'm guessing there's some kind of bad stuff happening with all the corn. You know, it wasn't just Hakim's father in Africa who had trouble. I think this corn problem may be happening all over the bloody world. Remember Wan Tin told us that even the small farms near her town in China were having problems this year. And my dad's been on the phone all the time. I can tell from his voice he's plenty worried.*

Well thanks, Roo.

No problem, mate, but why'd you ask? You seem concerned.

Not sure yet, but I'll let you know.

You'll be right, mate?

Yeah, see you, Marco answered.

Marco scurried around the computer's search engine one more time. He was looking for news: news about corn, news about bugs, *any* news that might hint at the story. But there was no news at all. He took a deep breath, furrowed his brows, and went to work.

He got out the information booklet that he was given at the Chicago Board of Trade.

"Hmm, let's see," he said to himself. He took a clean piece of paper, and at the top he simply wrote: <u>C O R N</u>

Then he put down all the facts he knew:

CORN

1   One contract of corn cost $600 to trade. This is called "margin money."

2   I have $10,000 in my account and $10,000 ÷ $600 = 16.666. So I can buy 16 contracts. That will cost me $9600 (16 x $600) and I'll have a little money left over to pay for the exchange fees, which is for all the record keeping done by the Board of Trade.

3   If corn goes up 1 penny, one contract will earn $50. But I will have 16 contracts (16 x $50=$800), so each penny increase in the price will earn me $800.

4   The LIMIT amount, or the maximum amount that corn can move in one direction in one day, is 20 cents.

5   If a one penny move earns me $800, a twenty cent move, a LIMIT move, would earn me $16,000 (20 x $800 = $16,000). Yes, if corn goes LIMIT up, I could earn $16,000.

Next, Marco went to the White and Garrett Brokerage Firm website, careful to make sure there were two "r's" and two "t's" in Garrett's name. He found the page for trading commodities, and he wrote 16 when the order form asked for the numbers of contracts.

Then the form asked for the type of order. He thought, *Got to be careful to choose Limit. I want that specific price, and only that price.*

"Now, let's see. I think I'll enter $2.20. That was the price at which corn had closed for the last two days. Yeah, it must be an important number."

The screen flashed a preview of the order:

The Account Number	#DEH 1018
Action	BUY
Number of Contracts	16
Commodity	CORN
Type of Order	LIMIT
Price	$2.20

Then Marco again read from his information booklet: "Corn trades on the Futures Markets quite literally in the future. A farmer will hedge, or sell in advance, on the Futures Market at a certain price to protect his profit and limit his risk."

Marco continued reading.

"A speculator, or trader, will take the risk if he feels he knows what will happen to the price of corn."

Now, thought Marco. *This is November. I'll choose December Corn. I think that would be the best month to trade. After all, a move in corn is going to happen soon or it's not going to move at all.*

Next, the screen asked him to preview the order. He hit the appropriate button. A new page lit up:

ORDER	Account #DEH 1018
BUY	16 Contracts of Dec. Corn @ $2.20
MARGIN	$9600

PLACE ORDER

Marco hit the 'place order' button. The next screen lit up: ORDER ENTERED

He waited. He didn't move. He just stared at the screen. The market hadn't opened yet, but Marco glowered at the screen. The room seemed quiet, painfully quiet. But his mind wasn't. In fact, there were so many thoughts racing around in his head that he was actually relieved when his mother shattered the silence by calling to him.

"Marco, where are you? Your breakfast is getting cold, and you don't want to be late for school, do you?"

One last thought jumped into his head, a most devious thought. *Now, if I were sick, nothing life threatening, but something pretty serious, Mom would make me stay home. I could have this fierce sore throat and a fever of about two-hundred degrees or something. Joey said he used that one once and his Mom fell for it. Now, what did he say he did? Right, he put the thermometer close to a hot light bulb. Wonder how long you do that? Nah, Mom would probably find out I'm faking it anyway.*

Suddenly, he realized a forgotten fact, an important fact; he was hungry.

"Hey, Mom," he called out while racing down the stairs, "have you got any of that strawberry shortcake left over from dinner?"

"Marco, for breakfast?" She shook her head. "Sometimes you amaze me."

"Sometimes I even amaze myself," he said, parking himself at the breakfast table and sporting an outrageous smile.

"Marco, are you up to something?" said Lilly. "Bet you are. I can always tell."

27

"Showtime," whispered Marco. "Now if I could just get my heart to quit pounding."

Ramon, Ramon, Ramon

CONFRONTING MARCO AS HE ENTERED THE SCHOOL lunchroom was a crowd of kids in what looked like a tight huddle or an overgrown beehive.

Just then, the center of the hive came alive. As it sprung open, out popped Joey.

"Marco, did you hear what happened?" he said. "We saw Ramon on TV."

"You saw Ramon?" said Marco. "How in the world did you *see* Ramon?"

"In social studies class."

"I saw him, too, Marco," said Piper, breaking away from the huddle.

Surprisingly, the whole group moved sideways as if it were one entity. The center now moved around Marco.

"Okay, not all at once," he said. "Just tell me what's going on."

"You know how Ms. Evlin has us watch the news from all over the world? Well, this morning, there he was."

"There who was? Einstein, do me a favor. Fill me in before I lose my mind."

"Marco, I don't know anything more than you. I'm in *your* class, remember? We don't meet until after lunch."

"So Joey," said Marco, turning to his buddy, "what gives?"

"Ramon!" said Joey, his voice rising an octave. "It was Ramon. We saw him on TV."

"That's what you've already told me, but could you fill me in on a few details?"

"In Ms. Evlin's class," said Joey, trying desperately to regain his composure. "You know, she shows us those news clips from time to time. News from strange places."

"Yeah," said Marco. "But mostly they're last night's news from the BBC in England. The other foreign news is usually old stuff."

"Right, and I asked her how she does it," said Einstein. "She told me she records them from home. Logical enough. Should have thought of that myself."

"But this was a *live* broadcast," said Joey. "I'm telling you, I saw Ramon. I'm not kidding. I saw Ramon."

"How do you know it was Ramon?"

"He was flashing all ten fingers," said Piper. "Joey's right, Marco. He gave the Marco Polo Blackberry & Company signal. He was holding both hands up in the air and opening his fists. It was very clear—all ten fingers!"

"Well, what did they say? What did the people being interviewed say?"

"I dunno," said Joey.

"What do you mean you don't know?" said Marco, raising his voice.

206

"Keep your cool, Marco," said Piper. "Everybody was so excited to see Ramon that some kids were shouting at the TV. Even Ms. Evlin wanted to know what this was all about. She was thrilled to learn that Ramon was Joey's pen-pal. I told her that some of us were trying to help kids in trouble. She really liked that idea."

"But didn't anyone hear what was being said?"

"Are you kidding?" said Caree who was standing alongside Piper. "With all the whooping and shouting, we couldn't even hear the teacher."

"Damn," said Marco under his breath.

"Hey, Marco, don't sweat it," said Einstein. "We'll catch it all this afternoon, in our 2:15 social studies class."

✲ ✲ ✲

Mr. Carr, the science teacher, was in top form during Marco's 1:30 class. While Marco was usually riveted by the fascinating world of flora and fauna, at this moment he had no idea if Mr. Carr had said that whales or sharks are fish. In fact, if his teacher had mentioned that his sleeve was on fire, Marco would not have heard.

"Marco," called Mr. Carr, "why are sharks referred to as 'swimming computers?'"

Fingers tapping, Marco looked up and said, "Swimming companions?"

"Well, sharks might indeed make charming *swimming companions,*" said Mr. Carr, "but that's not the topic right now. Tell me Marco, just where in the world are you at this moment? You don't appear to be in science class."

"You're right about that," he mumbled under his breath, looking down at his book.

"Okay then," said Mr. Carr. "Let's hear from Albert. Perhaps *you*, at least, are tuned in this afternoon."

Einstein looked over to Marco and Marco nodded.

"Well," Einstein said, "sharks are referred to as the 'swimming computer' because of the six senses they possess: vision, hearing, vibration, smell, taste, and electro-perception."

Marco turned his head to peak at the wall clock at the back of the room and then turned back to his open book. Peek, *two* minutes after two, turn; peek, *three* minutes after two, turn; peek, *four* minutes after two, turn.

"So for homework," said Mr. Carr, "I'd like you all to research these six senses of the shark. Write a report detailing…"

Marco jumped as the buzzer suddenly brought the proceedings to a close.

"Remember class," said Mr. Carr, trying to talk over the hurley-burly of scraping chairs and end-of-class chatter. "We need to know why each of the senses is valuable to the shark."

"Hey wait up, Marco," said Einstein. "I'm coming." Finally catching up just outside Ms. Evlin's classroom, Einstein asked between gasps, "What's the urgency?"

"Do you know that the only reason Ramon was on TV was that his father was being interviewed?"

"Yeah, so…"

"Well, he's the head of one of the biggest corn growers associations," continued Marco.

"And…"

"And the announcement he made could be very important."

"Oh, why's that?" asked Einstein.

Marco shook his head. "I'll tell you later," he said. "It's just very important right now that I see that video."

As they entered the classroom, Ms. Evlin was beginning to issue her typical opening remarks: "Class, settle down. We have a lot of things to cover this period. First, let's review the homework."

Marco, dry-mouthed, drummed on his desk while his teacher droned on and on about the annual rainfall during the African monsoon season.

What if I made a gigantic mistake when I placed the order to buy all those corn contracts? He wondered. *Sometimes computer information just disappears. Suppose* White and Garrett *never got my order. Or worse, what if they did get my order and I was wrong about the corn. Maybe all the adults already know about the problem and it's no big deal.*

No, he told himself, *it is a big deal. If bugs are eating the corn, it is a very big deal!*

He remembered how workers from Uncle Horace's farm had complained about the "dancing corn." *Bet those little buggers were chomping away right then.*

"So, Marco," said Ms. Evlin, "how did you respond to question nine, the number of countries in Central America?"

"Beg your pardon?" said Marco, looking up at his teacher.

"Seven," whispered Einstein from the seat behind him.

"Seven," said Marco.

"And they would be?" she added.

Marco looked back with blank look.

"Ooh, ooh," moaned Einstein from the seat behind. He was frantically waving his hand.

"All right, then," said Ms. Evlin, "do you want to give it a try, Albert?"

"Belize, Costa Rica, El Salvador, Guatemala, Honduras, Nicaragua and Panama," chanted Einstein.

Ah Einstein, thought Marco, *you saved my tail again. Thank you, thank you.*

Marco was quite sure that the ensuing class discussion was going to last until summer vacation.

Finally, Ms. Evlin went to her desk and opened the laptop computer. She made sure the connections were correct and the images were projecting onto the large screen in the front of the room.

"Showtime," whispered Marco. "Now then, if I could just get my heart to quit pounding…"

"Where's that tapping coming from," said Ms. Evlin. "Whoever is doing that tapping, would he or she kindly stop?"

Einstein's hand reached from the seat behind and latched onto Marco's arm. He gave it a squeeze. Marco didn't realize that he himself was the culprit.

"First, we'll have the BBC report from London."

Marco's sigh was loud enough to provoke a look in his direction by the teacher.

Several news reports came on the screen in one foreign language or other, the English translation scrolling below.

"Now then, class," said Ms. Evlin. "We have a special treat. One of the... there's that tapping again. Whoever is doing that tapping, will you kindly stop?"

Marco felt his face redden. He grabbed his right hand with his left, as if he needed some external force to stop those fingers that were moving apparently all by themselves.

"Now," she began again. "One of your classmates from another section actually saw his pen-pal on television. We were looking for a live station from a country in South America; the time zones are similar to ours. Argentina is three hours ahead of us, so our nine o'clock section was able to get the live twelve o'clock noon news."

The teacher told the class what Joey had said about the Marco Polo Blackberry & Company kids communicating with other young people around the world.

"Marco, I understand that you started this blog. Perhaps you would like to tell the class what it's all about."

"No, not really, Ms. Evlin. I mean not at this time. I don't want to be rude, but could I do that another time?"

"Of course," she said. "And now my eager young students, here's that news report from Argentina. It was live this morning, so I saved it for this section."

Everyone was sitting on the edge of his seats as the announcer, speaking in Spanish, said "El presidente de Argentina propone un nuevo programa de salud para ustedes..." and scrolling beneath in English were the words, "The Argentine president proposes a new health initiative...

Marco tried to get a good look. The translation written in English at the bottom of the screen was very fuzzy. He squinted, trying to bring the print into focus.

Just then, a burst of whispering swirled around the room.

"There he is," said one kid who had heard about the news report at lunchtime.

Ms. Evlin, seeing the excitement, told those in the back of the room to come up front.

"No pushing, everyone," she said. "You will all get to see."

Suddenly, several members of the class started chanting, "Ra-mon, Ra-mon, Ra-mon." Sure enough, Marco could see his friend standing near the man who was speaking into what looked to be a dozen microphones.

The boy was flashing all ten fingers. "Atta boy, Ramon," said Marco under his breath. Someone was poking his arm. It was Einstein, nodding with great vigor.

Marco strained to see the translation on the bottom of the screen but Stu was blocking his view. Stu stood almost six-feet tall and was the center of the basketball team. Marco was out of luck.

In desperation, he stood on his chair. Snaking across the bottom of the screen he saw: "...and so thank you, Mr. Diaz, for enlightening us about this corn situation. And now, another newly breaking story..."

The scene faded from view but the chant, "Ra-mon, Ra-mon, Ra-mon" continued to resonate through the classroom.

"Einstein," said Marco, his voice suggesting a note of desperation, "what did the scroll say? Could you read it? What did this Mr. Diaz say?"

"Dunno," said Einstein. "I couldn't see either. That Stu Forester takes up a whole lot of space."

The class ended with the usual surge for the door. Marco heard someone say, "boy, Joey's so lucky seeing his pen-pal on the news. How cool is that?"

✷ ✷ ✷

T-Bone was waiting as usual, his tail wagging at high speed as soon as he saw Marco lumber down the school steps.

Marco crouched down, scratched the dog behind the ears, and gave him a big hug, a gesture that evoked a wet *schlurp* across his cheek.

"You're a good ol' dog," he said, drying his face with his hand. "Give me five." The dog obediently lifted his left paw.

"Marco," said Einstein walking over, "what's with you today? You've been really weird all day."

"I have *not* been weird," said Marco. "I just have a lot of things on my mind. Listen, I've got to get home quickly, so I'm going to run ahead. See you tomorrow."

Lilly was riding her new pink bicycle, with the training wheels, down the sidewalk in front of the house as Marco jogged up the driveway.

"Yo, Lilly," called Marco as he headed across the lawn into the house.

"I'm still mad at you, Marco. You never include me. You never tell me anything."

"Cause you're so little," said Marco. "When you get just a bit bigger, I'll tell you more grown up things."

Lilly stuck out her tongue, but Marco barely even noticed the insult. He ran into the kitchen and snatched two brownies from under the plastic-wrapped cookie plate. Then he bounded up the stairs, two at a time, slamming the door of his room.

He pressed the 'start' button. His computer began to cackle and hum. It practically said 'hello' to him as the screen lit up, and Marco replied, "Hi, ol' buddy," as if he were greeting an old acquaintance. Carefully he typed, "White and Garrett." When he reached the correct website, he entered his account number and password.

There it was: the statement that his order was filled. He had bought 16 contracts of corn at a price of $2.20, just as he requested.

Marco looked up today's price at the close of the market. The corn market is open from 8:30 AM to 1:15 PM, Central Standard Time. Marco looked at his desk clock: four o'clock. There on the screen was December Corn with a closing price of $2.40. Marco blinked, rubbed his eyes, and blinked again.

"Far out! How cool is this," he said aloud. "I bought in at $2.20 and now it's...wow...Limit up! *Amazing.*"

Marco tried to think. "The story must have gotten out on the Argentina news at noon. But it was nine o'clock here, Central Standard Time. My order went in when the market first opened at 8:30 AM. So I got that price. Boy, the 'corn pit' must have gone wild when the news hit."

Then he went all over the Internet. The story was exploding, Australia, South Africa, Japan, India, China; everywhere there was news and it was bad. The beetle infestation was evidently rampant.

All the reports indicated that the price of corn was going to skyrocket!

Marco leaned back in his chair, clasped his hands behind his neck, eyes sparkling as he look up and to the right.

Hmm, he thought, *snowboard or jet ski? Maybe I'll just get both. Yeah, but I've just have to have that All-Terrain Vehicle.*

He leaned over, grabbed a nearby brownie and took a huge bite. Some crumbs trickled down the front of his shirt, but he didn't notice.

28

Marco: "Corn crops all over the world are yelling, 'Help me! Help me!'"

Limit Up

ON TUESDAY, MARCO RUSHED HOME FROM SCHOOL, RAN INTO his room, and booted up his computer. CORN, Limit Up read the closing price on the website.

He immediately instant messaged Jean-Louis, his Canadian 'partner in crime.'

Howdy, wrote Jean-Louis. *Sup?*

I did it, good buddy! Marco typed out. *I bought sixteen contracts of corn.*

Sounds cool, but would you mind filling me in on this 'contract' business?

Oh, that's how it's traded. One contract of corn equals five thousand bushels. The important thing to remember is if the price of corn moves up one cent, I make fifty dollars for each contract. I put an order in to buy corn Monday morning before school. I got lucky because I bought it before the news came out. By the end of the day it was all over the TV.

What news?

Haven't you been watching television, Jean-Louis? The devastation of the corn crop; that's all they've been talking about. And so corn went Limit Up. And now it's Tuesday. Corn's been Limit Up for two days.

Damn, Marco, how much money did you say you're making each Limit Up day?

$16,000.

Give that to me again, wrote Jean-Louis. *$16,000 is the number that came up on my screen.*

That, my man, is literally what I made — sixteen thousand big ones.

I am speechless! But how long are you going to stay in the market? Big winners can become big losers very quickly.

You've got that right. When I was at the Chicago Board of Trade, a story came out that there weren't many soybeans around. Boy, did the traders go wild. Soybeans went up the limit. I was there. I saw it happen. Then everyone found out that it had been a rumor and it wasn't true. The market price turned around and dropped like a rock.

Brutal. But are you sure, really, really, sure that this one's for real?

Just check the news, Jean-Louis. It's on television, on all the channels. There's an insect that disguises itself as a kernel of corn and eats the real kernel, then multiplies. Then this little critter has lots and lots of babies and when the tykes are ready, off they go, looking for a kernel of corn all their own. Corn crops all over the world are yelling, 'Help me! Help me!'

Well, is there anything that you can think of that will make this corn market start to head down?

Ah, wise words from north of the border. You're right. I have some serious thinking to do.

If I come up with anything, I'll give you a heads-up," said Jean-Louis. *"Got to give you credit, Marco, you're gutsy. Talk later. Bye.*

✼ ✼ ✼

"Here, Marco," said Mother, handing her son his newly arrived computer magazine. "It just came in today's mail. Oh, and if you're headed upstairs, would you please tell your sister to wash up for dinner? We'll be eating as soon as Dad gets home, because I have a PTA meeting this evening."

"The mail?" said Marco. "Today?"

"Well, yes, it does come every afternoon around two."

The mail, he thought. *Darn, the mail! I almost forgot. The brokerage house will be sending a statement confirming the trade I made. Maybe they've already sent it and it's in Dad's pile! But I put the order in Monday and it's only Tuesday. It wouldn't get there that fast.*

Marco's mind raced ahead. *Tomorrow. That'll be the day. But how am I going to get out of school in time to be home by two o'clock? A stomach ache? No, if Mom's not home, they'll keep me chained up until someone's around to drive me home.*

The band, he thought suddenly. *Of course, the good old band. They get out early for practice on Wednesday afternoons. Joey's in the band. Maybe he could 'accidentally' leave his drum at home and I, his good friend, could volunteer to get it for him?*

Maybe not. Bad idea. First, they'd never fall for it. And even if they did, how would I get home the following day if the letter never arrived. How many drums could I volunteer to fetch for an old friend?

"Marco," said Mother. "I *did* ask you to go and tell Lilly to get ready for dinner, didn't I?"

Yes, Lilly! Why didn't I think of that? "You bet, Mom. I'll get her right away."

Taking the stairs two at a time, Marco stopped at the closed door. He took a deep breath and focused on the job ahead. He tapped on her door, calling out, "Oh Lilly, my lovely sister, Lilly. Can I come in?"

"You can get lost," said Lilly.

"Hey, that's no way to talk to your only brother."

"Well, that's how you talk to me," she replied.

"I'm sorry," said Marco. "But can I come in? I have something very important to ask you."

"All right. But I'm still mad at you."

Marco opened the door gently and peered in his sister's room. "Why are you mad?"

"You said T-Bone couldn't go for rides with me in my dolly stroller. He really likes to, you know."

"I'm not sure about that, but listen, Lilly, let me ask you something. You go to kindergarten every day, right?"

"Yes…"

"Mom picks you up at noon because you're in a half day program, right? What do you do after that?"

"Oh, I have lunch and then I go out and play, unless it's raining."

"Remember when you asked me to teach you how to tell time?"

"Yeah?"

"Well, after dinner I will."

"How come?" asked Lilly. She cocked her head. "Bet you want something from me."

"Aha, my little sister, you're not only pretty, but you're smart."

"So?"

"So I'd like you to be on the lookout for the mailman when he comes by the house. That would be around two o'clock. I want you to get the mail, look for a certain envelope and when you find it, put it in my desk drawer. I'll show you what the letter looks like; I have one from the last time they wrote to me, and the new one will just look like the old one."

"Who's the 'they'?"

"It's not necessary for you to know," said Marco.

"Oh yeah, then it's not necessary for me to get the letter for you. Anyway, you don't allow me to go into your room if you're not there."

"All right, all right," said Marco. "It's a letter from a company saying that I bought something."

"Don't you know if you bought something?"

"Sure I do, but this is just a confirmation. You know, they kind of say, 'Right, you bought it.'"

"What'd ya buy?" asked Lilly.

"Just some contracts of corn," Marco said.

"Why'd you want those?"

"Enough!" said Marco, narrowing his eyes, his voice growing louder.

"All right," said Lilly, "but you're going to have to promise that I can wheel T-Bone around in my dolly stroller."

"Yeah, yeah," said Marco reluctantly. "But only before four o'clock. I don't want any of my friends seeing him."

"And," said Lilly glancing over, her eyes beginning to dance, "I want to be able to dress him up in my dolly clothes with a bonnet."

"No, that's a definite *no*," said Marco. "No play clothes, no bonnet."

"All right, get the mail yourself," she said in a soft voice, smiling sweetly. Lilly knew when she was holding the winning lottery ticket.

Marco sighed and then said, "Okay, you can put a hat on him. But no other clothes, and the dog has to go back to looking like a dog by four o'clock. Deal?"

"Deal," said Lilly, her teeth visible as the sides of her mouth widened.

✡ ✡ ✡

Sure enough, on Wednesday, just before two o'clock, Lilly positioned herself on the bottom step of the front porch. Right alongside of her was T-Bone, sitting in Lilly's doll stroller, wearing Marco's red baseball cap. Marco had conceded to that, as it was certainly better than a pink dolly bonnet.

"Hi there," said one of the neighbors, walking past the house.

The woman stopped and gave Lilly and T-Bone a long look. One couldn't help noticing this most unusual twosome.

"Doesn't your dog look handsome."

"Yep," replied Lilly. "T-Bone and I are waiting for the mailman."

The mailman arrived only a few minutes later, almost exactly at two o'clock. "What a greeting I'm getting today," he said to Lilly. "To what do I owe this wonderful welcome?"

"I'm helping out," said Lilly. "I am going to collect the mail today."

"Good for you, young lady." And with that, he put a packet of magazines and letters in her hand.

"Thank you," she said as she began to sort through the pile.

"I didn't know that you could read," said the mailman.

"Well, actually I can't. I can only read one kind of letter." After taking a moment to look, she pulled a letter out of the pile. "This one," she said, waving the White and Garrett Brokerage Firm letter in the air while flashing a broad smile. "Bye! C'mon T-Bone, we've got to go in."

29

Limit Down

WEDNESDAY WAS ALSO A LIMIT UP DAY. BACK HOME AFTER school, Marco opened his computer, logged on to the 'Marco Polo Blackberry & Company' blog and quickly broadcast his triumph to Jean-Louis.

You've got to be kidding. Marco, do you realize you're rich!

Hi guys, said Roo joining the conversation. *How rich?*

He's making mega money, trading in the commodity markets, said Jean-Louis. *Have you thought about what you're going to do with all that money? I think I'd go for that All-Terrain Vehicle. You should buy one for each of your friends too!*

Plasma screen TV, wrote Roo. *With all that lolly, I know I certainly could use one of those.*

Just then, Wan Ting, from China, logged on. *Marco, you really are wonderful.*

A regular wonder boy, that's me.

No, I'm serious. Don't you realize you've saved lives, Marco? Piper has been telling me about the shipment to Africa, and then she posted some of those letters.

Oh yeah, the letters. They were cool, weren't they?

I particularly liked the one from Mallaki, where she wrote, 'We have nothing, no family... We feel so sad. Then the truck came.' Marco, that was terrific! I also felt good that I could help in some small way with the netting.

Not a small way, Wan Ting. Hakim said that the rainy season had already begun. Those nets could make a big difference.

Hey, Wan Ting, said Jean-Louis. *Did you know our friend Marco here has been at it again, making money? Roo thinks he ought to buy a plasma TV. I'm for the All-Terrain Vehicle or maybe the snowboard. We get a lot of snow here in Canada. What do you think?*

I only want to study hard and learn much. So I guess I won't have the need, Marco, for those things you mentioned, said Wan Ting. *I must bicycle twenty kilometers to get to the big city three times a week to go to the technical school. But I am very fortunate because it is in the city that I can get on the Internet. If I should ever have such money as you, there are many people that I would like to help.*

The computer screen went quiet. For an uncharacteristically long period of time, there was no new writing. No one was saying anything. Then Jean-Louis broke the impasse. *Sorry, Wan Ting,* he said.

Sometimes we spend so much time concentrating on ourselves that we forget that much of the world isn't having one big fat party. Come to think of it, I can get on really well without a stupid All-Terrain Vehicle.

Yeah, said Roo. *I was just kidding about the plasma TV. I don't really feel good about it. I don't need that thing either.*

While Jean-Louis, Roo, and Wan Ting were chatting, Marco watched the conversation scroll by on the screen.

Then he remembered the picture of the African girl, the one that Mrs. Brown had given him–so young. He reached into his bottom desk drawer and pulled out the slightly faded photo of that half-naked little girl with the dark empty eyes. He studied the picture. *Sad, sad eyes, he thought; eyes without hope.*

I came online today, continued Wan Ting, *because I told some friends about this group, Marco Polo Blackberry & Company and about your efforts to help the children in Africa. Several of them volunteered to make more netting on their own time. In fact, they already have; we now have many bundles of netting. Where should we send them?*

Yeah, wrote Piper who had just joined the group. *My friends all know about what happened in Africa. Everyone wants to help. Any ideas?*

Marco, Roo broke into the chat. *We haven't heard much from you. You're very quiet. What's going on?*

Well, I've been racking my brains here, replied Marco. *Roo, your dad's company, donated grain; that was cool, and he put the X-ray machines and our packages on the plane to Africa, which was actually incredible. But as you said, his company can't keep doing that. Mr. Gardner, the guy who gave us those X-ray machines, said pretty much the same thing. We can't continue to count on those companies to donate stuff forever. So it occurred to me that what we need is money, and lots of it! Everybody should come up with a plan, a way to raise money.*

Well, said Jean-Louis. *For starts, I could chip in the money I've been saving for my own flat screened TV. I don't really need one. I have almost $125. Tell me where to send it.*

I'll donate my babysitting money, offered Piper. *It won't be a lot, but it's something. Hey wait, I have an idea. I might be able to get some of my friends to set up a bake sale. We could sell cookies to the neighbors.*

Now you're thinking, said Marco. *Keep the ideas coming.*

I've seen some of the older kids raise money for their class trips by washing cars at the parking lot of the high school, said Jean-Louis. *My friends and I could do that.*

Way cool, said Joey who had just joined in the conversation. *Marco, we could wash a few cars at our school, too. Just get some soap, pails, sponges and rags, and some garden hoses to hook up to the outside faucet of the school. We guys could wash the cars and then the girls could make some big signs that we could put up around town.*

Excuse me, Joey, said Piper. *Hate to break it to you, but girls can be as good at washing cars as the guys. That actually sounds like more fun.*

Hey, guys, said Marco. *Let's not argue. We need everybody's efforts. Unfortunately this problem is big, way, way bigger than we realized.*

Ciao, Marco, it's me, Stefania. I have some news for you from Italy. I know it sounds unbelievable, but Alfred, Marta's brother—you know, the fellow you helped get out of jail, well, he's coming to the United States, to Illinois. What do you think of that!

How is that possible?

Dr. Furlano, the doctor he's been working for, invited him to come to this big international conference. It will be in a city called, Champaign, IL. Isn't that near your town? Alfred is very smart and he speaks English. He would be a sort of assistant for the doctor.

Do you know what conference it is? asked Marco.

I think it has something to do with agriculture and science."

How does the <u>International Scientific Conference on Pests in Agriculture</u> sound?

Bravo! That's it. How did you know?

Just so happens my uncle is one of the people organizing the event.

They're probably in the United States already. I know Dr. Furlano is presenting his paper this Friday morning.

Wait a minute, didn't you tell me that Dr. Furlano was working with a brilliant American doctor? Does the name Dr. Brody, sound familiar?

Si, I think so, said Stefania. *But how did you get that name?*

My uncle mentioned him, said Marco. *Tell me, Stefania, can you remember anything that Alfred said about this trip? This could be terribly important!*

Well, he was very excited. He mentioned something about a big problem with bugs that the doctor was working on with his American colleague. The two doctors will make a joint presentation at the conference.

And he was happy? Not just happy to be going on a trip, but super happy with what the doctor found out?

Si, I mean, yes, I think so.

Wow, this could be big, said Marco. *Thanks, Stefania. Got to go.*

✵ ✵ ✵

Well into the night, Marco read every news item he could find about the corn blight. Sure enough, all accounts indicated that there was no corn out there. News items even appeared which reported that much of the world was nearing a state of panic.

"Beetles have infested the corn all over the country," was the gist of every report Marco scanned. "The effect," the newscasts stated, "could be far-reaching, impacting farmers, the economy, even the world food situation."

This bug is some kind of menace, thought Marco. Then he found the website of the agricultural conference. Looking down the page, he read the time, dates, and names of the universities and companies that were sponsoring the program. Reading further, Marco saw that the association president would be delivering opening remarks at 8:30 AM. At 9:00 the first paper was to be presented and at 10:00 AM., a panel of four experts would discuss the merits of a new kind of rice seed that was reportedly fast growing but bland tasting.

Just what the world needs most, thought Marco, *lots of tasteless rice.* Reading on, he found the following program:

11 O'CLOCK, FRIDAY MORNING:

The presentation of a scientific paper,

co-authored by Dr. T.T.T. Brody, from

The United States and Dr. L. Furlano, from Italy.

Staring at the webpage, Marco tried to think about what his inner North Star was telling him. Auntie M. had said, "Whenever you are conflicted as to what is the right thing to do, just take a deep breath and feel inside. It's a way of listening to your own inner North Star. If what you are about to do gives you that feeling of a warm smile, then you know it's the right way to proceed."

Marco's bed covers managed to end up precisely where he didn't want them as he tossed and turned the night away. When he awoke, he felt exhausted; and yet, at the same time, he felt distinctly calm.

It was Thursday morning, and he had made his decision.

Before school, Marco took a deep breath, thought carefully, and put an order in to sell his entire position for 20 cents higher than last night's price. He placed his order for $3.00.

Corn could go up limit at least another day, he thought, what with all the lousy news. If you believe the press, there will never be corn again, ever.

Yep, Marco thought. Time to get out.

✵ ✵ ✵

Thursday afternoon, Marco's sprint home from school would have broken all existing records. And inevitably, in his rush to get his computer up and running, he pressed all the wrong keys.

"Teeny steps," he scolded himself. Finally, there it was in bold letters at the White and Garrett website:

ORDER FILLED: $3.00

He noticed the balance on his account. It read:

Account: # DEH 1018

Current Balance: $68,000.47

Marco stared and stared at the figure on the screen. He rubbed his eyes. He thought maybe it would disappear, but the figure remained precisely as he had first seen it. Then he heard Lilly talking to Mother outside his bedroom door. He quickly closed his computer.

Thursday night Marco did his five math problems without bothering to check his answers, skimmed a poem by Robert Frost, and dashed off a paragraph which would probably not fill his English teacher with joy. Then, knowing what he faced, he cleared his mind of all the stuff that wasn't vital. At exactly nine o'clock, he opened the second drawer of his desk. There they were: all the booklets with information on commodity trading that he had kept from his visit to the Chicago Board of Trade.

He read them twice. Going "short" on a commodity was a new concept, and Marco wanted to make sure he had it right. Using the money that he had made on his "long" positions, when the price went up, Marco figured out that he could now trade 110 contracts of corn on the "short side." He took out a clean piece of paper and wrote down the number: $68,000. Then he figured that if it took $600 of margin money (the money required to trade one contract) he could purchase at least 110 contracts on the "short side" with some money left over. He continued: $68,000 ÷ $600 = 113.33

"Careful now, Marco," he said aloud. "Got to leave some money in the account to pay exchange fees and stuff."

Next he wrote: 110 contracts times $600 per contract equals $66,000 or (110 x $600 = $66,000)

Neat business, this commodity trading, he thought. You make money when the price of corn goes up, and you can make just as much if the price goes down if...

Marco knew from his visit to the Chicago Board of Trade that if you take a "short" position, you are basically rooting for the price of the commodity—in this case, corn—to go down. You would "sell" the contract, "go short," and then "buy" it back at a lower price, if you were right. That "if" loomed large, though – *if* you were right.

He looked over at the pile of news items he had printed. He read them and then re-read them. *I'll bet there isn't a commodity trader alive that doesn't know corn is in a bad way.*

For the next half hour, he used several different search engines to find any sites that had information about corn.

"Nothing new," he said out loud, shaking his head. *Hmm, if everyone knows that there isn't going to be any corn, if they think it's all ruined, and then someone comes out with some good news about the crisis, as in— we know how to kill the beetles and save the corn—then yes, there'll be corn, and lots of it. Now, when you have lots of something, where would the price almost* have *to go? Down. That's right, straight down!* "'Short's' the word, Marco Polo Blackberry."

✻ ✻ ✻

The eastern sky was just beginning to grow light when Marco opened his eyes Friday morning. He stumbled to the bathroom, brushed his teeth in record time, splashed cold water on his face, and then went straight to his computer. Checking some of the websites that he had saved from last night, he realized the only new item was an article about the possibility of this corn-killing beetle jumping from the corn to the wheat crop or maybe the potato crop. It was all doom and all gloom. Marco closed his eyes. What to do? He thought again about his Auntie M.

"The answer lies inside of you, Marco. Just sit quietly and listen. It's really quite simple. Think what's right from your heart, and you'll have your answer."

Marco sat quietly and listened. Marco felt deep down inside. Then he placed his trade.

    ✻ ✻ ✻

At the end of the school day, the dismissal bell rang. Marco bolted out of the building so fast that he stumbled on the three little steps that led down to the pathway, practically knocking over T-Bone, who was loyally waiting for him. No time for a proper greeting. Marco just ran as fast as he could, T-Bone at his side. The poor dog couldn't quite figure out what was going on, but he did think this new racing game was great fun.

Marco sprinted into the house, taking the stairs two at a time. With lightning speed, he was on his computer. The news was all over the Internet.

"Scientists Have Developed the Antidote; Bye Bye, Beetles," read one article. "The Corn Crop Is Back," read another headline. Skimming the article further, he learned, "The new chemical would be used in spray form and would not damage the crop, only kill the insect."

Marco leaned forward towards the screen and slowly re-read the entire article. *Nothing has really changed,* he thought. *It was only the knowledge that a cure had been found. It might take many weeks, even months, to make and distribute the spray and then kill the beetles. How will the markets handle this?*

Carefully Marco opened up the White and Garrett website. He entered his password, held his breath, and stared at the computer screen. He attempted to exhale and instead a soft whistle floated out of his mouth. There it was, clear as could be. The screen read:

ACCOUNT: #DEH 1018

SOLD   110 Contracts December CORN

PRICE $3.20

Marco was puzzled for a moment; as he had put his order in for $3.00, last night's closing price. He quickly went to the website that had all the commodity prices. Yes indeed, the high price of the day was $3.20.

He returned to the news articles. They were all written in the afternoon, well after the scientific papers were presented. The Corn Market, he remembered, opens every weekday at 8:30 but the scientific paper wasn't presented until 11:00.

Friday morning, there was no news, so the corn prices opened again at LIMIT UP, twenty cents more than last night's closing price. Marco's order was automatically filled at $3.20, the Limit-Up price. He quickly took out his information booklet, "The Basics of Trading Commodities," and thumbed through. He read the section on Limits: "CORN, in one day could trade a maximum of twenty cents above the previous day's closing price, LIMIT UP; or twenty cents below the previous day's closing price, LIMIT DOWN."

He couldn't believe his eyes. The news had come out, and the price of corn dropped like a rock. It dropped forty cents! By Friday afternoon the price of corn had closed at $2.80. It had gone up limit and down limit in one day.

"Unbelievable!" he uttered to no one in particular.

30

…then a whimpering noise came from the doll carriage. The "baby" sat up, skirt, pink ribbons, doll bonnet and all.

The Parade

IT WAS SATURDAY MORNING AND AFTER BREAKFAST MARCO ensconced himself in his room. He opened every website and read every article he could find about this "scientific breakthrough." *The big world seems to be shrinking before my eye. Everyone knows everything about everything: Africans know that Pakistan beat England in a cricket match; Australians know the Amazon's flooding in Brazil; and I wouldn't be surprised if everyone in China knows what I had for dinner.*

A knock at his door interrupted his thinking. It was Lilly. His annoying little sister had arrived.

"Marco," she called out. "Come look outside!"

"Look at what?" he sighed. "What is it?"

"Don't you want to see the school band? They're marching right in front of our house. C'mon., we're all going to watch. Don't you want to see?"

"Too busy."

Out came the calculator. "Let's see," he mumbled. "If the price of corn goes down again, say on Monday, yeah…I'd make…hmm…but if it also went down on Tuesday, then…"

He closed his calculator and began tapping his fingers on his desk. He had so much on his mind.

Then too, he worried that the kids were asking where to send all the money they raised. He didn't know what to tell them. Piper suggested that the money might be mailed to her house. Her dad was a banker, and she felt sure he could help set up a special account.

The strains of John Philip Sousa's *Washington Post* filled the air while Marco was very deep in thought. The window in front of his desk only afforded a view of the parade if he crooked his neck to the right and looked far to the left. He could barely make out the first line of band players coming down the street. *It may only be the Saturday dress rehearsal for the Thanksgiving Day parade, but wow, that band sounds pretty good.*

Grabbing his jacket, he hurried downstairs to join his father, who was standing on the side walk looking around for Mother and Lilly.

The marching band, looking striking in their blue uniforms with white trim, and gold epaulets on the shoulders, was made up mostly of high school students; but there was always room for a few willing musicians from middle school.

They stopped momentarily down the street, evidently taking some last minute directions from the band leader. Then with a tentative bleat from the brass section and a hardy boom from the bass drums, the band moved off smartly, coming ever nearer to where Marco and his father were standing.

As he pointed toward the marching group, Marco called out, "Hey, Dad, there's Joey."

"Can't see him. Which one?"

"Over there. Tall skinny guy with the bass drum."

The booming sound of the percussions rose to a crescendo. Marco started waving both of his arms, like a sailor performing semaphore signals, in the direction of the band.

Almost every one of the players was marching in step.

Marco saw Joey look in his direction, perhaps nodding in recognition, but he couldn't be sure because Joey's oversized hat kept sliding down his forehead. The drummer next to Joey was Hank, the seventh grader who always seemed attached to Bart's shirttails.

"Big jerk," Marco mumbled. "But I've got to admit *even he* looks good in that uniform."

Just then, Mother came by with Lilly, who was pushing her doll carriage.

"Look at my dolly," said Lilly. "Look, Marco, see how cute he is!"

"Later," said Marco as the band was approaching.

"Now stay," said Lilly. "Be a good baby."

Marco heard barking in the distance and then a whimpering noise coming from the doll carriage.

The "baby" sat up – skirt, ribbons, pink doll bonnet, and all. Marco's mouth dropped.

There was his poor dog, dressed in doll clothes, girl baby doll clothes. T-Bone began emitting un-baby like growls. Across the street his old nemesis, Buckey, Bart's dog, was standing rigid, nose pointed forward, eyes glaring straight ahead. A cacophony of musical and canine sounds filled the air as T-Bone leapt from Lilly's carriage and ran directly into the oncoming parade, doll clothes dragging on the ground behind him. The pink bonnet, though, with streaming ribbons, remained securely fastened to T-Bone's head.

Marco made a mad dash after his dog into the street, trying to catch him while swerving through and around the band players. As T-Bone darted directly in front of the percussion section, one of the snare drummers leapt backwards, tripped, and landed with a wicked thud on the pavement. Marco, in hot pursuit of T-Bone, took a big dive trying frantically to seize his elusive mutt. What he came up with instead was a shocking pink doll skirt that had been hanging underneath the dog.

The marcher directly behind the drummer also took a tumble when T-Bone, now totally confused, made a U-turn back into the middle of the parade. Marco again made a desperate grab and this time managed to take hold of the dog by the collar, but not, however, before six more band members went tumbling. There were several scraped knees, a rather severely dented trumpet, and a drum stick, broken in two.

"What the devil is going on?" shouted the bandleader.

"Sorry about that, fellas," Marco said lamely to the group of band players standing around. "You okay?"

Bart's sidekick, Hank, was sprawled on the ground next to the fellow with the dented trumpet. He stared angrily at him.

"You, the clown," said the bandleader looking over at Marco. "Who the hell *are* you? If your intention was to totally ruin our parade practice, you were unbelievably successful. What's your name?" he asked.

Bart's dog, standing on the opposite side of the street, let out a deep throaty rumble. With a sudden lurch, he wriggled out of his collar and jumped into the middle of the fray, going directly for T-Bone. Bart ran after him.

"Young man, I asked you, your name?" the bandleader repeated.

At the time, Marco was struggling to keep hold of T-Bone, who was not pleased with the situation.

"Marco Blackberry," offered Bart, who just appeared holding his dog with one hand while adjusting his dog's collar and leash with the other.

"I didn't ask you," said the teacher, "but is that your dog?" He pointed to Buckey.

"Yeah," said Bart.

"So what's *your* name?" asked the teacher.

"Bart McHugh, but his dog started it."

"No, he didn't," said Marco. "Your dog was barking at T-Bone from across the street."

"Yeah, well, you watch it. That dog's gonna be steak! And by the way, he looks like a weirdo. I mean, any dog that wears a pink bonnet..."

As the verbal exchange heated up, a shrill whistle pierced the air. The band teacher had blown it as hard as he could. He scowled at both boys. "So you're both in middle school. Well, I'll be speaking to your principal; and trust me, you can both count on staying after school for detention on Monday."

Somehow the band composed itself and continued on its way. Holding tightly to T-Bone, Marco waited till the parade finished before crossing the street to where his parents were.

"I'm going to kill you," he said when he saw his little sister. "What did you do to my dog?"

"I thought he looked cute in my doll clothes," she said. "And he's always behaved very well before. He likes to play 'dress up.'"

"You mean you've done this before? If anybody sees him..."

"Don't worry, Marco, I'll tell them that they are not your doll clothes, they're mine."

"What?" shouted Marco. "Mom, you've got to *do* something!"

31

"So what's the lesson that you learned?" asked Lilly.
"To never get detention again," said Marco.

Detention

THE NOTE FROM THE PRINCIPAL WAS TAPED TO MARCO'S locker: *Marco Polo Blackberry – Report to Mr. Henry's office at the end of school today, 3:00 p.m.. You are to be assigned to detention hall.*

Marco bit his lip, then shrugged. He had known it was coming.

"Hey," said Einstein, meeting him in the hall. "Who died? Or is it something you ate?"

"Worse," said Marco. "I'm in trouble. Big time."

"What?"

"I've got detention and I've just got to get home. I wonder how long I'm gonna be locked up."

"Hey, Marco," shouted Bart as they passed each other in the corridor. "You're a jerk, you know. That damn dog of yours got me into trouble. I've got detention. And you're creepy, dressing your dog up in doll's clothing."

Marco started after him and was ready to tackle him right there in the hallway if it weren't for Joey and Einstein holding him back.

"Hi there, Coach Chuckowski," said Joey in his choirboy voice as he noticed the coach coming down the hall. He had immediately released Marco who quickly became cognizant of the situation. Marco straightened the book bag on his shoulder.

"The Chucker" glanced around, his brows drawing closer together as he passed by.

Meanwhile Bart had managed to vanish.

"So what are you going to do?" asked Joey as the boys continued on to their next class.

"Haven't a clue," said Marco.

"Let's talk tonight," said Einstein. "See ya."

✳ ✳ ✳

Just before the dismissal bell, Marco received another note from the principal's office. This one read: *Marco Polo Blackberry – Your scheduled detention today has been postponed until tomorrow, Tuesday.*

"Darn," Marco whispered with such vehemence that several kids standing nearby glanced over. "Just when you think things can't get any worse…"

When he got home, he didn't head for the kitchen as usual. Instead he scanned the stack of mail sitting on the hall table. There was nothing. He knew it was too soon, too soon. But tomorrow…for sure, it would come tomorrow.

He grabbed an oatmeal cookie, munching as he went up the stairs at his usual clip, two steps at a time. As soon as he was in his room, he put on his headphones. A big smile appeared on his face as the sound of his favorite music broadcast through his MP3 player. He listened for a moment.

Then he took a deep breath. He slid his laptop in front of him, furrowed his brow and went to work.

Ah, there it is, the web-site for the brokerage firm.

When he saw the price of corn for the day, he let out a loud, "Yes, yes!" and punched his fist in the air.

Sure enough, corn had dropped again to $2.60, Down Limit. Marco searched around the Internet, reading everything that he could find. All the news articles were full of the excitement over the cure for the beetle blight. There were even reports of people cheering and dancing in the streets. Marco was tempted to do a little cheering and dancing himself.

"Oh, you mighty gods of the trading floor," he said outloud, "just one more day. One more day of 'Down Limit' and…"

He sat for a moment, tilted his head slightly left and glanced upward. *When corn went 'up Limit' it did so for a full four days,* he thought. *I think this thing could trade 'Down Limit' at least one more day, which would make it the third day of 'Down Limit.'*

He put his order in to include one more down day, the entire limit. Tomorrow he would close out his position at $2.40.

"Lilly," Marco called, walking out of his room and down the hall. He knocked politely on her bedroom door. "Can I come in?"

"You can come in if you watch where you're walking," said Lilly from her bedroom.

As he entered, he noticed what seemed to be every doll and all the doll clothes that Lilly ever owned strewn all over the floor. The dolls were in various stages of undress.

"Oh, sister dear," Marco sighed.

"Want to play?" she offered, looking up at him.

"No, I don't think so, but I *do* need a favor from you."

"Well, I don't know. Not too long ago you wanted to kill me. That's not very nice."

"Oh, Lilly, you know I really didn't mean it, but you got me in so much trouble. I've even got detention after school tomorrow."

"What's tention?"

"It's *de*tention and that's when the principal makes you stay after school for maybe an hour or more to teach you a lesson."

"What's the lesson that you learned?" asked Lilly.

"To never get detention again," he said. "So, do you think you could meet the mailman Tuesday like you did before, and get the White and Garrett letter for me?"

"Is that the one that I can read all by myself?" she asked.

"Absolutely, that's the one. So…?"

After pausing for a moment, Lilly looked up and said, "No."

"No?" said Marco, his voice rising. "I do so much for you and here I ask you for a little favor…"

"I would if I could, but I can't, so I won't," Lilly sang out.

"What do you mean you can't?"

"Well, it will be Tuesday, right?"

"Right."

"On Tuesday I have ballet lessons. I'm a regular ballerina, and I get to wear my pink tutu. Want to see?"

"Sure, but not now," said Marco, his voice back to its normal pitch. He walked out of the room shaking his head. Once on his computer he went to the Marco Polo Blackberry & Company site and noticed Jean-Louis already talking with Joey.

Hey, guys.

What's up, Marco? answered Jean-Louis.

Do you want the good news first or the bad news?

The good stuff for sure.

Okay. Corn went Down Limit again today and I'm making big-time money.

Awesome, answered Jean-Louis.

Definitely, Joey added. *So what's the bad news?*

I have to stay after school tomorrow, Tuesday, instead of today, Marco typed out in reply. *And I'm sure Tuesday will be the big day. But even worse, the brokerage statement from White and Garrett should be arriving in the mail by then, and guess who won't be home to receive it? Talk about feeling bummed out.*

Can't you get Lilly to pick it up for you again? asked Joey.

I wish, but she's going to some dumb ballerina class tomorrow afternoon. I'm dead, dead in the water, if I don't get to the mail before my parents. I don't know, grounded-for-life is a real possibility.

Hey, Marco, wrote Jean-Louis. *You knew you're going to have to tell them eventually. Didn't you think about what you'd say?*

I guess not. I mean I haven't thought it through. I really was going to say something to them. But then I thought I'd wait till my Dad was in a good mood to approach him. I was going to tell him everything I learned about what's going on in the world: you know, the wars, the sickness, the kids without parents. And I was going to tell him especially about Hakim's problems. I've been doing some thinking. I've decided whatever money I make from all this trading, well; it's going to the kids, all those kids who have had their lives turned upside down. I know it's only a start, but I have to do something.

Marco Polo Blackberry, that's really awesome, came Jean-Louis's reply.

Well, my aunt, Auntie M., always tells me that if you don't have the guts to try stuff, you'll never change any of the things that really need changing. She's a wise lady, and I believe her about that changing stuff. But right now, I'm worried. I'm going to have change and get some new parents.

32

The Jig Is Up

"LILLY, YOU LOOK SO SWEET IN THAT TUTU," SAID HER mother, but why didn't you change into your regular clothes before leaving the dance studio?"

"You said we were going to meet Auntie M. at the train station, and I wanted her to see me all dressed up."

"Well I'm sure she'll think you look wonderful."

Lilly's eyes sparkled, "Think so?"

Mother slipped into a parking space right in front of the station just as the train pulled in.

"There she is!" shouted Lilly, leaping out of the car, and waving wildly.

"Auntie M., over here. We're over here."

Auntie M. stopped in front of her niece, arms spread wide as Lilly ran into her embrace. "I can't believe it! You look, well, you look like a beautiful fairy, just ravishing. But tell me, what *are* you wearing? It appears to be so magical."

Lilly giggled. "It's a tutu. And I'm a ballerina."

As they reached the car, Auntie M. opened the car door, and with a grand gesture, said, "Jump into the carriage, my fairy princess."

Lilly hopped into the car, pink and red ribbons bobbing up and down as she bounced in her seat.

While driving home, Lilly commented, "Guess the mailman has already come."

"I certainly hope so. He's usually here by two o'clock," said her mother. "But why are you interested all of a sudden?"

"Oh, I have to pick up a letter for Marco."

Mother turned her head quickly and gave Lilly one of those looks only mothers can manage.

✡ ✡ ✡

When they reached home and the car stopped, Lilly leapt out before her mother had even taken the key out. The five-year-old made a beeline for the mail box.

"Yep," she said thumbing through the pile of mail. "Here it is. This is the one."

Mother looked quizzically at her daughter. "Now why would a little girl who does not yet read get so excited about a letter?"

"Yes, I can *too* read," said Lilly. "I can read just one kind of letter and this is it." She waved the envelope around above her head. "Marco taught me how."

"Please give me that envelope Lilly," said her mother, hand outstretched.

Lilly did so without lifting her head. She recognized that tone. A twig on the ground in front of her had suddenly taken on an incredible fascination.

As they walked inside the house, Mrs. Blackberry started reading the contents of the envelope. Her eyes grew wide as she saw a brokerage statement with a confirmation for a closing "buy order" of 110 contracts of corn placed last Friday. She didn't understand the language, but what she did know was that large sums of money were involved. Without putting the statement down, she reached for the phone.

"Hello, Mark?" she said to her husband. "Have you been trading in the markets on the Internet again? I have a letter here from the White and Garrett Brokerage Firm."

"Of course not," said Mark Blackberry. "I told you I was finished with that stuff."

"But do you still have your account?"

"I don't know. Maybe they keep it open for a while in case you want to go back to trading. Why are you asking?"

"Well, a brokerage statement arrived, confirming a trade for corn contracts. There was a *huge* amount of money involved. All I know is that something is going on. Marco had asked Lilly to get the envelope for him."

"Marco? Oh gosh. Is he there?"

"He had detention after school today, so I'm expecting him to be delayed."

"Margaret, I'm on my way home. Be there in ten minutes. You call the school and tell them it is an emergency, and we want Marco to come directly home."

✿ ✿ ✿

"Hey, T-Bone, ol' buddy," said Marco. The dog was waiting outside the school door. "Well, the jig is up. We're dead. I mean, I'm dead. Mom called the school. Do you know what the principal said to me? He said, 'Young man, your parents called. You are to go home immediately. Do you understand? Immediately!'"

He looked down at T-Bone, who as usual responded by wagging his tail.

"Can you imagine that? Do you think they allow prisoners to have dogs in jail?"

T-Bone stared at Marco, his oversized floppy ears reaching down his cheeks almost to his jaw. He cocked his head to the side, looking up at his master as if he understood. Then, standing up on his hind legs, he gave a big wet kiss with his tongue across Marco's face. Returning to the ground, he raced around and around the boy in circles. In spite of himself, Marco laughed out loud.

"Listen, T-Bone. I really didn't mean *not* to tell them. I don't know what happened. I just got…caught up in it, ya know?" He kicked what he thought was a rock in front of him on the path. "Ow," he called out, rubbing his toe.

T-Bone ran to see what it was. He sniffed the brick, and finding it of no interest, once again took his place at Marco's side. Then he barked twice, his "have you got a treat?" bark.

"Yeah, I know; you want a cookie. But I don't have one. You know, you're probably my best friend in the whole world. In fact, very soon you may be my *only* friend. I'm really sorry, big guy. I mean about the cookie. I guess it's not your day either."

He stopped for a moment to reach down and rub his foot. "It didn't seem that wrong," he said, "all that trading. The money was going to be for poor kids. Well, actually, at one time I guess I did think about that plasma TV and the All-Terrain Vehicle and all assorted kinds of goodies. But, that stupid urge didn't last very long. Once I found out what was happening in the world— Hakim can't even go to school, villages getting raided, no food, no medicine, people getting killed..."

The dog looked up at Marco and again tilted his head.

"I tell ya, T-Bone, the world can be a real mean place, especially for kids."

✧ ✧ ✧

Marco opened the front door and walked slowly into the foyer, T-Bone at his side. Looking first at his mother and then at his father, he felt the need to swallow but found that task uncommonly difficult. Then he saw Auntie M., and what might have been a faint smile crossed her face.

"Marco," said his father, holding up the letter, "I do believe you have some explaining to do. First off, speak up, speak clearly, and I want the absolute truth. Do you understand me?"

"Um…er…I don't know where to begin," said Marco, teeth clenched, eyes darting from one parent to the other. He was trying to read the expression on his father's face. It occurred to him that his parents looked like those cartoon characters who get so excited that smoke comes out of their ears.

"Marco," said Auntie M. "do you remember I read the story *Alice in Wonderland* to you when you were younger?"

He nodded.

"Well, why not do just as Alice did when she was asked to explain what happened. It's really quite simple. Begin at the beginning, and when you come to the end, you can just stop."

"Okay," said Marco, drawing a deep breath. "It all began when Jean-Louis and I ran away from camp and found that goldmine. We overheard some men talking about a new valuable gold strike."

"You ran away from camp?" said Mother. "I never knew that!"

"Well, sort of, I mean, not really. Actually, it was just for a few hours and we came back. No one knew we had even gone, so it's kind of like we never left. And then after camp, the 'White and Garrett' letter came and it was addressed to me. I know it was probably a mistake but…"

"*A mistake?*" said his father.

"Mark, calm down," said Auntie M. "Let's hear the whole story. Continue Marco."

"So that's how I got started– buying this goldmine stock. Then with the money I made, I bought corn contracts in the commodity market because I knew about the corn problem before it came out in the news. Once the news broke, everyone thought there would be no corn since the beetles were eating all the kernels. After that the price of corn just skyrocketed."

Marco continued to tell them about his pen-pal, Roo, from Australia, when he was interrupted by the door bell ringing. Mark Blackberry's mouth, which had been opening wider and wider as Marco's story continued, snapped shut at the sound. He answered the door.

Standing there sporting enormous smiles were Mr. Warren Garrett and Mr. Jonathan White. Mark recognized them from the brokerage firm. Mr. White extended his hand.

"Let me be the first to congratulate you," he said.

"Jonathan White here." "And let me be the second," said Warren Garrett, squeezing Mark Blackberry's fingers so hard that Mark had to fight back a grimace.

"That was some of the shrewdest trading that I've ever seen," said Jonathan White.

"Yep, a brilliant piece of work," added Mr. Garrett.

"Well, to tell the truth," Mark Blackberry said, "I didn't make those trades."

"No?" Mr. White said, leaning forward.

"No, it was my son, Marco, over there."

"*You did it?*" said Mr. White, eyebrows raised as he looked at the young boy.

"He was just explaining the whole thing to us," said Mr. Blackberry. "Why don't you have a seat?"

Marco began again. When he got to the part about the X-ray machine, Mr. Garrett stopped him.

"Do you know a Mr. Gardner, Mr. Daniel Gardner?"

"Yeah, that was his name," said Marco, "the man who gave us the X-ray machines."

"I can't believe this. *You're* the kid? Danny Gardner's my brother-in-law. He told me all about this kid who raised money for medical supplies for some town in Africa. Oh my word!"

"Listen," interrupted Mr. Blackberry. "I hope you're not going to press charges. My son hasn't had his thirteenth birthday yet. I'll take full responsibility."

"Press charges? No, no, of course not. Well, I guess this check is for you then," said Warren Garrett, handing it to Marco. "It's over a half million dollars!"

Marco looked at the check for a moment and then gave it to his father. He looked up at Mr. White and Mr. Garrett.

A small grin appeared on his face. "Guess corn was Down Limit again today," he said, his eyes beaming, "and I got out at my price."

"You better believe it," said Jonathan White. "It is incredible, $540,000. That was the best trading I've ever seen. So what are you going to do with all that money?"

Marco looked at his father, who stared at the check, turning it over twice.

"I don't want any of it for me," said Marco. "You see, there's this village in Africa that was burnt to the ground and…." As his story unfolded, those in the room listened intently and remained silent.

When Marco finished his tale, Mark Blackberry's expression was no longer grim. It could best be described as a look of bewilderment.

After Messrs. White and Garrett left, Mr. Blackberry turned to Marco. "You and I will have a talk later this evening."

That night at dinner, Marco had difficulty eating anything. And what he did eat seemed to get stuck in his throat. In fact, a piece of food, which he was sure, must be the size of a golf ball, sort of stopped midway. It took a full glass of water to get it down. After that Marco swore off food.

The next day Auntie M. called him aside. "So what was the verdict?"

"Well," he said. "I'm grounded for four weeks—of course, that really means only weekends—but still it hurts. No TV for a month and the use of the computer for only one hour a day—they know I sometimes have to use it for my homework. Also, I have to keep my grades up and, oh yes, no more allowance until, well, until they decide differently."

"Marco, I know you had some good intentions," said Auntie M. "What you and your friends did was remarkable, and I know you did it with a good heart. But you went a bit too far, doing all those things without telling your parents. Not such a good idea. But look, I spoke to your father last night. Your dad and I agreed that we'd turn the money over to a banking friend of mine who would set up a trust fund so we could put that money to use.

Marco stared at his aunt.

"And then I wondered," she continued, "who do I know that might have some good ideas about where to send the money, you know, so that it will do the most good? I mean, I really could use some help deciding. Do you suppose I could count on you?" She reached over and gave his hand a tender squeeze.

Marco looked up at Auntie M., who was gently nodding. She had a soft smile on her face as her eyes sparkled. And so did his.

33

The Biggest Smile of All

Six Months Later

"LET'S GO MARCO," SAID MARGARET BLACKBERRY. "OF ALL
the nights not to be late, this is the one."

"No, Lilly, T-Bone is not going to accompany us to the awards dinner. He
will remain home, as usual."

"Why not?" asked Lilly. "He told me he'd love to go. Wouldn't you?" She
looked straight at the dog.

T-Bone cocked his head and looked from Lilly to Mrs. Blackberry and
back again.

"All set," said Marco, bounding down the stairs, lucky red shirt visible
under his navy jacket.

"You look so nice," said Mother, "but if I could suggest, maybe you could
give a little more work to some of that hair sticking up in back."

Without missing a beat, Marco ran back upstairs to the bathroom. He grabbed the large brush on the shelf above the sink. Slapping water on top of his head and vigorously worked to tame the beast.

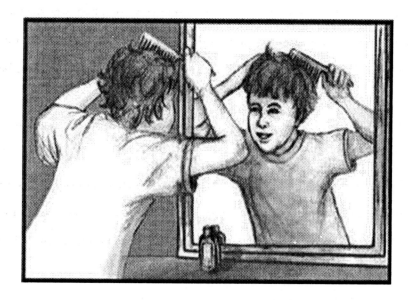

He smiled at the mirror. "Pretty good," he said to the reflection.

✵ ✵ ✵

As the Blackberrys entered the high school auditorium, Marco stopped for a moment to survey the scene.

"C'mon," called his father. "If we don't grab seats now, we'll be scattered all over the place."

Amazing, thought Marco. It's not just the middle school. Looks like everybody in town is here *but* T-Bone.

Up on the dais sat none other than Donald Relleh, mayor of the town of Lizbeth. Seated next to him was the deputy mayor, the town administrator, and further down, the chief of police resplendent in full dress uniform. Also on the stage was a man Marco didn't know, but later found out was the managing editor of *The Clarion*, Lizbeth's local newspaper. In fact, Marco hadn't a clue why most of the men and women on the dais were so important, but apparently they did.

"I pledge allegiance to the flag of the United States of America and to the republic..."

Then the speeches began: some long, some short, and most, Marco was quite sure, he'd never remember. Interspersed were a few musical renditions from the high school band. He spotted his dad looking at his watch and stifling a yawn.

"This is very boring," said Lilly.

"Hush," said Mother.

She does have a point, thought Marco.

"And now," said the Mayor Relleh, as he stood in front of the podium, "The moment we've all been waiting for: the presentation of the 'Outstanding Young Person Award.'"

"Ta-dah," Marco whispered.

"As most of you know, by giving this award, we recognize a young individual who inspires and motivates us all. A person who excels in his or her chosen field and exemplifies the best attributes of the young people of Lizbet."

The mayor cleared his throat, and Marco leaned forward in his chair, his heart racing.

"And so," the mayor continued, "it is with enormous pleasure that I, Mayor Donald Relleh, present this award to Bart McHugh, of the Benjamin Franklin Middle School, for his outstanding athletic skills and good sportsmanship. He has almost single-handedly catapulted our town into the State Middle School Championships and, might I add, for the very first time. Bart, Bart McHugh, would you come up here?"

The crowd burst into applause. Marco, however, sat there in stunned silence, his mouth open in disbelief. His dad looked over at him and patted him on the knee.

When all was quiet again, the Mayor stood beaming, as if he had just announced that one of his very own citizens had landed on the moon. Bart came forth, head bowed, in what apparently was an attempt to look modest.

"Young man," said the mayor as he shook Bart's hand. "Let me present you with this plaque as 'Outstanding Young Person' and this certificate of recognition of your superior leadership talent."

Again, applause filled the auditorium, and this time Marco politely joined in.

Several moments later, Marco was aware of his father calling, "Come on, family. Let's see if we can't get to the cafeteria before there are big crowds."

At the reception, Mark and Margaret Blackberry went over to talk to Bart and his parents.

"Pete, Amy, congratulations! How proud you must be."

262

"Heck, you *bet* we are proud of our boy," said Pete McHugh. "Hey Mark, did you see that final game, the one that clinched the title? I heard Coach Ski called Bart an inspiration in the locker room afterwards. 'Showed great leadership!' That's what he said: 'great leadership.' I'll tell ya, Mark, fortitude and hard work brings its own rewards. That's what I've always taught Bart. You wait and see, just got to toughen your Marco up a bit. He too might make a name for himself someday."

✳ ✳ ✳

Saturday morning after the awards ceremony, Marco's father saw his son in the den working on a jigsaw puzzle.

"Can you spare a minute?" he asked, entering the room.

"Sure, Dad," Marco replied as he settled himself on the leather sofa. "What's up?"

"About last night..."

Marco held up his hand. "It's okay, Dad. I'm cool with it."

Mark Blackberry smiled. "That's good son, real good. But it does seem, well, I just wondered how much thought that committee put into deciding this year's winner. I know you must feel disappointed."

"Maybe a little," Marco said, "but not too much. Besides, what in the world would I do with that awful plaque?"

His father laughed as he came over and tussled his son's hair. "Then you really are all right with it?"

"Truly, Dad."

His father nodded, and as he got up to leave, he said, "Oh, I almost forgot. This came for you in the mail." He handed him a letter.

Marco opened the envelope, which was covered across the top with exotic stamps. A picture was enclosed, showing his friend, Hakim, the other school children, and their teacher standing in front of a small grey building which looked like it had a brand new tiled roof. He put the photo in his pocket.

Dear Marco,

We can't thank you enough for all the wonderful help. Because of you and your friends, we were able to put on this fine new roof on our school. Notice the extra strong construction of the thatching and roof tiles. Best in the area! We now have money to pay for Mrs. Goma's salary and enough left over to buy new books and a lot of writing supplies. Mrs. Goma loves her new chalkboard. Malika wanted me to tell you that for the first time she has hope. Someday she wants to be a teacher. She's the one in the front row on the far right; the girl wearing the yellow dress with three small buttons. I'm standing just behind her. We owe you so much, Marco.

Your friend,

Hakim

✲ ✲ ✲

A short while later, the doorbell rang.

"Marco, it's for you," called his father.

Marco went to the front door. There stood Piper, her long curly hair gently pulled back on either side.

"I came to show you this," she said, handing him a magazine which was folded in half. "My father subscribes to the *United Nations Health Innovations Journal*. He pointed this article out to me. I thought you might like to see it. Here, it's from their 'News Around the World' section. You can keep it if you like."

Looking at him for a long moment, Piper added in a quiet voice, "I think you're wonderful Marco."

At that point she leaned toward him and planted a slightly moist kiss on his cheek. Turning quickly she walked away, her grey pleated skirt swinging behind her.

Marco just stood there, watching her for a while, his ears tingling. He put his hand up to his face which was beginning to turn red. *She looks a little different today*, he thought.

He went inside, closed the door, and then started to read the journal article:

Three hospitals in southeastern Africa have been the recipients of new X-ray machines and water filtration systems. A traveling nurse's initiative also set up vaccination programs for the prevention of measles in those surrounding areas.

The equipment and the money for all these supplies were sent by some
school children from a small town near Chicago, Illinois, in the United
States of America. The impact on the health care of these local people
was immediate and measurable. A spokesman for one of the hospitals
said, "Those areas being served will reap the benefit for years to come.
We hope this will spur other communities to aid our continuing attempt
to wipe out measles in..."

"Dad," Marco said, "There's something I'd like to show you." As his father walked over, he handed the journal to him.

When Mr. Blackberry finished reading, he turned to Marco. "Well, son, you should feel very good about yourself, award or no award. I'm so very proud of you." He put his arm around Marco, gave him a big hug, and then left him to his thoughts.

Marco took a deep breath and sat down. Slowly he read and re-read the article. Then he reached into his pocket and took out the picture of Hakim standing in front of the schoolhouse with the fine new roof.

Looking more carefully, he noticed that all the children were standing proud and tall and sporting wide grins. He looked for the girl in the yellow dress with three little buttons. Right behind her was his friend, Hakim, a tall skinny kid wearing the biggest smile of all. *A doctor, huh?* he thought. He tilted his head slightly and gazed upward. Then his eyes started to gently close. "Yeah, I can see that," he said, smiling and nodding to the empty room.

THE END

Acknowledgements

Almost halfway around the world in India lives one of my most ardent supporters and dearest of friends, Madhvi. Come to think of it with the advent of Skype she lives within my home and most surely within my heart as we chat for hours at a time.

She has given me practical advice, ideas as well as strategies. Most importantly she's my cheerleader extraordinaire, encouraging me to reach for the stars. I suspect with her spiritual nature she does have special powers; so I listen most carefully. Madhvi, you are indeed wonderful.

APPENDICES

Appendix A

100 WORDS OF INTEREST

Adjacent, adj   Close to, lying near

Agrarian, adj   Related to the land

Array, n   An impressive display

Ascending, v   Rising or going up

Bailing, v   Scooping water from a boat

Biohazard, n   A risk to human health or the environment

Bland, adv   Lacking strong qualities

Cacophony, n   A mixture of loud unpleasant sounds

Cadence, n   The beat, rhythm or tempo

Caftan, n   A full length tunic or robe

Chaos, n   Disorder, confusion

Cognizant, adj   Having knowledge of something, aware

Coiffed, v   Highly styled hair

Cowlick, n   A tuft of hair growing in a different direction

Dais, n	Raised platform at the end of a large hall
Decontamination,	adj System to remove unwanted chemical, radio-active or biological toxins
Disembarked, v	Get off passenger vehicle
Donned, v	Put on, throw on
Electro-perception, n	The ability to detect electrical fields, used by the shark to locate their food and explore environment
Emir, n	An Islamic religious leader
Encryption, n	The conversion of information into code
Entomologist, n	One who studies insects
Entourage, n	Special people who go with high ranking person on visits
Epaulet, n	Ornamental shoulder piece worn on uniforms
Fare, n	Food that is provided especially when simple
Femur, n	Main bone in the human thigh or leg of an animal
Flailing, v	Thrashing or swinging around
Fray, n	Exciting or energetic situation or activity
Funeral bier, n	Table or wooden frame that holds a coffin
Gaggle of geese, n	Flock or group of geese
Gangplanks, n	A movable walkway used when boarding a ship
Glowered, v	An angry or resentful stare
Grade (of gold), n	The quality and value of the metal

Guile, n	Cunning, deceitfulness
Gunwale, n	Top edge of a boats side
Hurley-burly, n	Turmoil, uproar, confusion
Inevitable, adj	Impossible to avoid
Infestation, n	The presence in large number of parasites that can cause damage or disease
Irate, adj	Feeling great anger
Jarring, v	Shaking something abruptly
Jostling, v	Knocking against others others
Laden, adj	Loaded, weighed down
Lament, n	Cry, expression of sadness
Loitering, v	Lingering, hanging around
Maharaja, n	An Indian prince
Mantra, n	A sacred word chant, or sound repeated during meditation
Marinated, v	Preserved, soaked
Massacre, n	Slaughter, mass murder
Mayhem, n	Disorder, confusion

Meandered, v	Wandered, roamed
Mesmerizing, v	Attention grabbing, compelling
Military time, n	A 24-hour clock, beginning at midnight, which is 0000 hours, and therefore 1:00 AM is 0100 hours, 2:00 AM is 0200,
Milling, v	To move around in a confused or restless group
Monsoons, n	Very heavy annual or semi annual rains
Mused, v	Considered, thought, mulled over
Myriad, adj	Countless, numerous
Nemesis, n	A bitter enemy, especially one who seems unbeatable
Obliterated, v	Erased without a trace
Oblivion, n	A state of being completely forgotten
Palate, n	A personal sense of taste and flavor
Pallor, n	Paleness, an unhealthy looking complexion
Palpable, adj	Able to be felt
Phenomenon, n	A fact or occurrence that can be observed
Precariously, adv	Dangerously, unstable, unsteady, insecure
Protrusion, n	Something that sticks out

Purification tablets, n	Tablets taken to get rid of something harmful, or unwanted contaminants
Queried, v	Questioned, asked
Quizzically, adv	Expressing question or doubting in a mocking way
Rabies, n	A severe viral disease, often fatal
Rappelling, v	Descending a steep slope using a rope harnessed that is placed around the body
Raucous, adj	Unpleasantly loud, noisy
Ravine, n	Deep narrow valley formed by running water
Recitation, n	Reading aloud or reciting something from memory
Regurgitate, v	To bring food up from the stomach
Resonated, v	To echo, to resound
Reverie, n	State of idle and pleasant contemplation
Ruddy, adv	With a healthy reddish glow
Sarcasm, n	Cutting language
Savanna, n	A flat grassland in a tropical or subtropical region
Sauntering, v	Walking at an easy unhurried pace
Scrunched, v	Squeezed something together tightly
Scurried, v	Moved briskly
Seismograph, n	Instrument that detects the presence of earthquakes

Semaphore signals, n	System of sending messages using hand held flags
Stevedore, n	Someone whose job it is to load and un load ships
Swaddled, v	Wrapped, bandaged restrained
Tarp, n	A canvas, cover, oilcloth
Torrents, n	A violent or tumultuous flow
Transfixed, v	Shocked or terrified so as to induce a momentary inability to move
Turmeric, n	A yellow spice made from a plant used in cooking
Tutu, n	Ballet dancers skirt, that is very short and made of layers of stiffened net
Unabated, adj	Still as forceful or intense as before
Ungainly, adj	Lacking grace
Unison, n	In perfect agreement or harmony
Unmitigated, adj	Absolute and unqualified
Uproarious, adj	Loud and boisterous
Vendor, n	Someone who sells something
Virtually, adv	Almost but not quite
Wailing, v	Mournful crying
Wok, n	Chinese cooking pan

Appendix B

GLOSSARY OF FOREIGN WORDS

Spanish

Bandito	A bandit; a thief
Caballos	Horses
El grano	Grain
El presidente de Argentina	The president of Argentina
propone un nuevo programa	is proposing a new health program
de salud para ustedes	for the health of all
Espantoso	Horrifying, appalling
Hola	Hello
Mi amigo	My friend

Australian

Bloody wizard	Very clever

G'day	Good day, hello
Good bloke	A good guy
Jolly good	That's great
Just smashing	That's wonderful
Lolly	Money
Mate	Pal, friend
Spot on	Exactly correct
Telly	Television, TV
That's a goer	That will happen for sure
Tyke	A youngster

Italian

Andiamo subito	We'll go right away
Ciao	Hello, hi
Grazie per tutti	Thank you for everything
Si	Yes

French

Beef bourguignon	A French recipe of a roast beef prepared with red wine and vegetables
Bienvenue au Canada	Welcome to Canada

Tutu	A short, pancake-like, many-layered tulle dance skirt
Voila	Used to call attention to or express satisfaction

Japanese

Ohayo, gozai masu	Good morning

Latin

Bonafide	Genuine; real

Appendix C

GLOSSARY OF TRADING TERMS

Account number- An individual number assigned by a financial institution for record keeping

Brokerage firm- A financial company that makes it possible for investors to buy, sell and trade stocks and commodities.

Brokerage account- A specific account held at a at brokerage firm

Brokerage website- A page on the Internet where one can access information from a brokerage firm.

Closing price- Price of a stock or commodity at the end of the day

Close position- To sell or buy back the stock or commodity, thus ending the trade

Commissions- The cost, the money that a person pays the brokerage house every time he or she buys or sells a stock

Commodities An unprocessed item that is bought and sold, such as corn, wheat, and soybeans

Commodity Exchange- Place where commodities are traded

Commodity market- Place where commodities are bought and sold

Commodity pits- A location in the floor of the exchange where groups of traders congregate to buy and sell commodities

Commodity trading- The buying and selling of authorized products on an exchange such as metals, agricultural products, petroleum, foreign currencies, to name a few.

Confirmation- The act of verifying that a purchase has been made.

Contract- Agreement to buy or sell a set amount of a commodity at predetermined price and date

Corn futures- Contracts to buy or sell a set amount of corn at a date in the future

Current balance- The sum total value of an account at the present time

Enter a limit order-	Place an order to buy or sell at a specific price, and only at that price
Exchange fees-	The costs of record keeping by a particular exchange
Filled- (as in a stock or commodity order)	A completed order
Futures markets-	Place for the trading of commodities in the future
Futures pits-	The location for the trading
Going short-	Selling a futures contract with the expectation to benefit as the price moves lower
Limit price-	A specific price desired
Limit amount- (or limit move)	The maximum a commodity can move above or below the previous day's closing price.
Limit Up/ Up Limit-	The maximum move above previous price
Limit Down/ Down Limit-	The maximum move below previous price
Margin money-	Money required to trade

Opening price-	Price of a stock or commodity at the beginning of the day
Soybean futures-	Contracts to buy/sell an amount of soybeans at a date future
Stock exchange-	Building used for trading stocks
Stock market-	Place for buyers and sellers to meet
Stock symbol-	Abbreviation that identifies a stock
Trader-	One who buys and sells stocks and commodities
Trading online-	The buying and selling of stocks and commodities on the Internet

Appendix D

Key To The Secret Code

MARCO POLO BLACKBERRY SECRET CODE

When you want to put a word into the secret code, use the next letter in the alphabet, with the exception of vowels. If you wish to use a vowel, choose the next vowel in alphabetical order.

Example: The word C-O-D-E would be written as D (for the C), U (for the O), F (for the D) and I (for the E).

Notice that you should skip over the vowels when writing consonants. The word 'Code' becomes 'Dufi'.

ALPHABET- QUICK REFERENCE

Consonants: b = c, c = d, d = f, f = g, g = h, h = j,

j= k, k = l, l = m, m = n, n = p, p = q,

q = r, r = s, s = t, t = v, v = w, w = x,

x = y, y = z, z = b

Vowels: a = e, e = i, i = o, o = u, u = a

Example: Marco Polo Blackberry

Nesdu Qumu Cmedlcissz